C000090892

TREGARTHUR'S LEGACY

Alex Mellanby

Cillian Press |

First published in Great Britain in 2018
by Cillian Press Limited. 83 Ducie Street, Manchester M1 2JQ
www.cillianpress.co.uk

Copyright © Alex Mellanby 2018

The right of Alex Mellanby to be identified as the Author of this work has been
asserted by him in accordance with the Copyright, Design and Patents Act 1988.

All rights reserved. No part of this publication may be reproduced, stored in a
retrieval system, or transmitted, in any form or by any means without the prior
written permission of the publisher, nor be otherwise circulated in any form of
binding or cover other than that in which it is published and without similar
condition being imposed on the subsequent purchaser.

British Library Cataloguing in Publication Data.
A catalogue record for this book is available from the British Library.

Paperback ISBN: 978-1-909776-22-7
eBook ISBN: 978-1-909776-23-4

Published by
Cillian Press – Manchester - 2018
www.cillianpress.co.uk

This book is dedicated, as before, to Pat Read and all the walkers who have and will take up the challenge of the Ten Tors. There is much to face out there, just hope you don't meet Miss Tregarthur.

Cillian Press are fantastic and have provided their expert touch as usual. It has been fantastic to have them ensure I keep on track, avoiding consistency errors that are so easy especially when moving in time.

Carolyn's has been essential with her perpetual re-reading, helpful critique and occasional bullying when my text became a machine-gunning of words, rather than sentences.

CONTENTS

PROLOGUE.......7

BROKEN TIME.......9

THE MAN.......15

BATTLE LINES.......22

MUD AND MORE MUD.......35

A MEDAL FOR JACK.......45

BLIND PANIC.......51

VISCOUNT HARPER.......59

SCOUTING PARTY.......69

BAYLOCK'S RUIN.......81

TROUBLE IN TIME.......96

THE ONLY WAY.......109

THE SEARCH BEGINS.......120

A MAN OF WAR.......134

NOT THE EASY WAY.......143

MEASLES.......153

BLUEPRINTS.......171

NO DEATHS.......181

THE SWAMP.......193

JACK'S BLUE.......207

ONE STONE.......220

EPILOGUE.......227

PROLOGUE

I am Alvin Carter, probably sixteen, but that might be sixteen thousand or more because I've been dragged unwillingly through so much history.

Once there were more of us. Now there are only three and Demelza only counts as one of the dangerous. Jenna and I couldn't stop Miss Tregarthur before. This time the danger is greater than our lives.

-1-

BROKEN TIME

They weren't shooting at us, it was worse than that.
When Demelza screamed, 'Get down,' the bullets whizzed over our heads. The planes were shooting at a band of shaggy looking, fur wearing, club wielding cavemen charging up the hill towards us. Miss Tregarthur had really made a mess of time.

In the seconds we had, I shouted, 'Run,' and we took off. Maybe we had thirty seconds, a few more after the planes returned, blasted the cavemen again, circled over us and then screamed off into the distance. Miss Tregarthur's time tunnel had brought the three of us to this bleak muddy hill. She said we deserved it. Cavemen and fighter jets. We knew this hill and this moor, the Hanging Stones always brought us here, the stones that showed the way through time.

'Make for the trees,' Jenna gasped and pointed. We were coming down from the hill, ahead was a wood of big Christmas trees, or whatever they are called. I turned. Behind us, the straggling wild men were chasing us down.

The jets had gone, but with a deep rhythmic 'chop-chop', a helicopter appeared, flying out from somewhere behind us. A loudspeaker blasted out: 'Halt. Stay exactly where you are.' That was followed by a stream of words I couldn't understand; a foreign language.

Demelza slowed down to look upwards. Jenna and I ran on, faster. The helicopter hadn't stopped the cavemen. We had no idea who was in the whirring machine, which started to buzz closer to us, continually calling out orders and adding threats to shoot. There was no way that I was going to stop and see what they would do.

I hoped Demelza might give us more time, even if she was torn apart by the savage tribe. That's something she definitely did deserve. I'd lost count of the times and ways she had tried to send us to our deaths. But Demelza came sprinting down to us. We jumped a wall and barged through thick and thorny undergrowth, finally finding a clump of trees which I hoped shielded us from the air.

Above, the helicopter turned and threw a smoking canister at the cavemen; green gas billowed out as it exploded. That did stop them and with howling cries they ran in the opposite direction. Then we heard the loudspeaker demanding that we come out of the wood. And another burst of strange words.

'Do we go out?' Demelza looked back to the open moor.

'Why don't you go out and meet them?' Jenna said. 'We'll watch and see what happens.'

Demelza didn't move. From our hiding place, we could see the pilot and one other man using the loudspeaker. Both were wearing military uniforms. We didn't move. The helicopter circled a few more times and then flew off.

'They'll be back, we need to move.' I stood up, looking for a way to go.

'Who? What? When?' Jenna groaned, knowing we had no answers.

We went on. From the hill, we had seen that the wood

wasn't that big, so we were bound to find the edge, provided we didn't go around in circles. We didn't have to worry about that because we soon came across a track. A track rutted with marks from huge vehicles. No choice, we pushed on.

'Whoa,' Jenna pulled me to a stop and we crouched down.

Ahead, a high wire fence closed off the track. There was no way through here. On the other side two soldiers were talking into their phones. We saw them unsling their weapons and stand ready, pointing them towards the wood.

'What's going on?' Demelza said in the whiney voice that had followed us for so long.

'Shhhh.' Jenna slapped her hand over Demelza's mouth and then whispered: 'We've no idea. I'm quite happy for you to get shot but perhaps you could just shut it.'

Demelza gave a Demelza face. It reminded me of how she behaved at school. She was the queen, her friends had to do everything she wanted. The rest of the school named her the queen bitch. Were we heading back to school times now?

The men with guns were patrolling this fence. They looked pretty much like ordinary soldiers. But only *pretty much*. I couldn't decide what was not quite ordinary about them. Somehow, they just weren't scary like soldiers should be. Were we in our own time? Had we returned? What had happened? The men moved off.

'I guess we have to walk round this fence until we find a way across.' Jenna stood up. 'Perhaps best if we ...' She stopped.

In front of us the bushes started moving. Not bushes at all, in seconds, we were surrounded by camouflaged soldiers, all with guns and all pointed at us.

11

'Halt. Handy hoe,' one of the soldiers shouted. He seemed to be in charge.

It was difficult not to laugh at the man struggling to say these words. He wasn't any older than me, none of them were. I suppose we should have been more scared – they were all armed – but so many scary things had happened to us before. I think we had become more than a little crazy. These soldiers just didn't look quite real. And I had no idea what they were saying but they kept repeating it.

'What are you on about?' I said when they seemed to be getting pretty cross.

'You speak English?' The lead soldier sounded amazed.

'Is that a problem?' Jenna replied. 'Are you going to shoot us or can we go?'

'This is a maximum restricted zone,' he said, coming to attention as we heard a vehicle approaching; an armoured vehicle with a large gun at the front.

'Caught them?' A man in a very smart uniform climbed out.

All the soldiers saluted. 'Yes, sir,' snapped the first lead soldier.

The new man started spouting at us in some incomprehensible language before turning to the other soldiers and telling them to put us in handcuffs. Even this man could only be a few years older than us. What was going on?

Jenna stepped forward. I knew she was going to do it, she always did when she got cross. She poked him in the chest. 'Look here, General,' she said. 'Just what is going on?'

The air was full of stifled sniggers.

'Major, actually.' We could all see he was trying to cling to his authority, it wasn't working. 'Cuff them,' he shouted.

'No, you don't.' I stood up next to Jenna. 'Not before you tell us what's happening and what's with the strange language.'

'Oh, you are good,' the Major sneered. 'Next you'll be telling us you really are English.'

'Strange you should say that.' Jenna was ready with another poke but the Major had moved backwards. 'Very strange,' she repeated. 'Because we are.'

'You are the German spies we have been waiting for.'

'Hang on,' Demelza joined in. '*They* may be your German spies, but I certainly am not.'

So Demelza was trying yet again to drop us into a mess. I had a feeling these people shot spies. It didn't seem as though they wanted to hear any more from us. They might be young but they were nervous and this was starting to feel more dangerous.

'Do what they say,' Jenna said quietly.

We were put in handcuffs and marched along the side of the fence until we came to a gate.

'Move it,' one of them said, listening to the familiar sound of the cavemen in the distance. It seemed a good idea to do what he said.

The gate was as high as the fence, with rolls of razor wire and a sign that said it was electrified. It opened, and we were pushed through, then the gate clanged shut behind us. A line of soldiers stood with their guns pointed into the wood. In the distance we saw more cavemen, whooping and howling. They didn't come any closer.

We were taken into a low brick building. It had to be army. A British flag drooped on a pole outside. On the side of the building a notice board carried pictures of men who were labelled as wanted and deserters. All the time these soldiers were snapping to attention, saluting, saying, 'Yes, sir,' as though their lives depended on it.

'This is bad,' Jenna said to me and was told to shut up.

Demelza was already trying to flirt with the Major.

A few steps into the building Jenna wrenched away from the guard. I could see why. At one side stood a purple coloured vending machine.

'Chocolate, give me chocolate,' Jenna started hammering on the machine.

Her guard looked confused and Jenna kept on getting louder and louder, shouting for chocolate. I could understand that. Cavemen, the Black Death, convict ships to Australia, radiation in France. Miss Tregarthur had sent us to so many places in so many different times, but never, not once had we had any chocolate. And it didn't look as though we were going to get any now.

2

THE MAN

They pushed us into a barred cell together. A dirty concrete room big enough for even more people. Iron bunk beds on one wall, bolted to the floor, with grey blankets and dirt stained pillows. Barred windows.

'I'm not using that.' Demelza screwed up her nose, pointing to the bucket in the corner.

Of course it was Jenna who fixed up blankets to screen the bucket, and in the end we all had to use it because they kept us there for two days. The food was awful – the sort of thing you might have cooked in some school cookery lesson; one where cabbage was the only certainty. More and more it felt like this was some sort of made-up attempt at being a military organisation, a school event without teachers.

We tried to ask what was going on and got nowhere. The person who brought the food looked about thirteen and very nervous. A second soldier, with a gun, stood right outside the cell; another teenager and even more nervous.

Jen gave me a questioning look, as though we might jump the food boy. I shook my head. The boy with the gun was jiggling from side to side, fingering it and he looked like he needed an emergency go with our toilet bucket. He looked like the sort of boy who might just start firing at anything. Might hit anyone.

'Back away,' I whispered, and we all moved away from the bars.

On the second day the two of them seemed a bit calmer until Jenna started on them.

'Oi, you with the damp trousers. What's going to happen to us?' Jenna asked.

The food boy looked down, checking.

'Shh, don't speak to them, you know the orders,' said the gun boy in a loud whisper.

'You've got to wait for the man.' The food lad almost tripped over his feet in the hurry to get away.

'What man?' we all said at once. The noise made the boy even more frantic and he managed to bang the bars shut with him on the wrong side. That made us laugh. Then the gun went off with enough recoil to knock the other boy off his feet. Lucky that the bullet just hammered into the ceiling. More soldiers arrived. This all felt stupid, not real, in a dangerous way. I could see all the soldiers were near to collapsing in giggles, laughing at the one who had fired his gun and looked like he might have wet himself. But the one who said he was the Major started shouting at them, before turning to us:

'You lot better not make trouble, or the next bullet will be for you.'

'Not before the Man arrives, eh?' Jenna taunted him. He turned red and marched off. After that they kept someone in the corridor outside the bars all the time. Another nervous boy with a gun who refused to talk, or get any chocolate which Jenna kept demanding.

On the third day, we heard several heavy vehicles roar into the compound outside.

'Do you have a very bad idea, about this man?' I said to

Jenna, who nodded with a groan.

Demelza started smoothing herself down, fluffing her hair, wiping her face. Demelza had guessed who it might be.

A group strode into the corridor space outside our cell.

'Surprise!' the Man said, puffing out his chest of medals.

Demelza went straight to the bars, 'Zach, get me out of here NOW.'

So, Zach, the school bully, murderer, coward, and every other bad thing you could imagine, Zach was *the Man*. It wasn't a surprise at all. Ever since we'd been thrown around in this mess of time travel, Zach had turned up in some important position – bailiff, judge, and now here as a military commander. He was wearing a fantastically well pressed uniform with shiny buttons and was surrounded by other shiny soldiers, all male, except one. The female soldier had almost as many medals and even more confidence. She whispered in Zach's ear and stood up right in front of Demelza.

'I do not think that the Supreme Commander is going to let you out,' she said and turned to Zach, who went bright red and shook his head. Demelza had been replaced. Zach had a new girlfriend.

Demelza went berserk. 'Supreme Commander, eh? Just get me out.' She grabbed hold of the bars, shook them and screamed, 'You can't leave me here.'

'Oh yes he can,' the female soldier smirked.

'It's almost worth being locked in here,' Jenna said quietly to me. 'Just to see Demelza get this, see her suffer.'

Demelza hadn't finished. She stopped screaming and said through clenched teeth: 'Zach, you have to let me out.'

Zach had turned away. One of the men with him raised his gun at Demelza. 'Call him sir, or you die.'

With that they moved off down the corridor. Demelza shouted, 'I know things about you. If you don't let me out ...'

The man who had raised his gun returned and smashed the butt of his gun through the bars into Demelza's stomach. She fell to the ground, gasping for air. The man grunted at her and left.

Some minutes later we heard the engines roar as Zach and his lot left the compound. It was hours before the Major returned. Demelza had taken to one of the beds, covered herself in blankets and done some wailing, some crying and some screaming about being betrayed. All of that made me feel just a little better.

The Major stood in front of us, you could see that Zach's visit had terrified him, but he had his orders – a pile of papers in his hand.

'Alvin Carter,' he was looking at one sheet. 'You will be taken to the front.'

He paused. The way he said it felt like a death sentence and I'd certainly heard those before.

'The other two of you will be sent to a farm.' The Major looked up. 'Tomorrow you leave.'

This had to be bad, very bad, because he leant forward and threw Jenna a bar of chocolate with an American name on it. Later they even gave us a newspaper.

'It's a war,' Jenna said, with a chocolate stained mouth as she read from the newspaper.

She'd given one small piece to Demelza, who had a face like

the worst of weather – worse than thunder, more like earthquake. From time to time Demelza repeated how she was going to kill Zach. I would have helped her, but doubted Zach's new soldier girlfriend would let Demelza get anywhere near him.

'What war?' I asked.

'It looks old.' Jenna held up the paper showing a picture of men in trenches, or actually boys, with loads of horses and mud. 'It reads as though everything is going Britain's way, but it sounds crazy, they say they made a two-foot advance yesterday – as though that's a big thing.'

'I guess I'm going to find out,' I said. 'At the front, in those trenches. That's where they're going to send me.' I poked my finger through the picture in the paper.

Another soldier appeared. 'Your uniform,' he said, passing me a heap of army clothes through the bars and throwing in a pair of boots. Heavy old khaki material, something I might have seen in an old film. I hadn't realised until then that all the soldiers were dressed in something similar, except Zach's lot who had been wearing more modern clothes. 'Make sure you put it on, tomorrow you'll need it.' Then he stomped off.

'There's no date.' Jenna shuffled the pages of the paper. 'What war is it? Have we any idea what year it is?'

'No idea,' I was picking through the army uniform pile wondering if I should put it on.

'Let me.' Demelza jumped up from the bed and grabbed the paper. She peered at it for a while before turning to us. 'The pictures look like the First World War.'

'Can't be,' Jenna puzzled. 'That vending machine, Zach's lot. Can't be the First World War still, it must have ended years …' She stopped and looked up.

'Yep,' Demelza scowled. 'It's has to be her, she's done it. Miss Tregarthur. She's messed up time, somehow the war is still going on and on. That's why the soldiers are all boys. The rest are dead.'

I understood now why we got the chocolate. It was a last wish. They didn't expect me to return from the front. There was no way out.

'I don't think it's real, even with the war, it isn't a real part of time.' Jenna was reading more of the paper. 'Seems like a mixture. Most of it seems stuck in the past.'

'Zach didn't seem stuck anywhere,' Demelza puffed and went red.

'Missing your boyfriend?' Jenna got in another dig.

'That would definitely be Miss Tregarthur,' I said, not wanting the two of them to start fighting. 'Mixing up, messing things and getting me killed.'

'I can't believe …' Demelza moaned but didn't finish.

'Can't believe what?' I stared at her. 'Can't believe Zach is a nasty, scheming, two faced coward? I thought you would have guessed that by now.' Demelza buried her head in an army blanket.

We went over things, again and again just as we'd done so many times in so many dangers and never found anything helpful. Jenna reckoned she was going to a farm. 'To grow more cabbage for the war effort. That's what it says in the paper. That's what all the women are doing.'

In the morning, I struggled into the uniform. It didn't fit well, but I could see that I needed something hard wearing if I was to be taken off into muddy trenches. They came for me, five of them, expecting trouble, but I couldn't see any point in trying to get away. There were too many, even if they were too young to be real soldiers. I hugged Jenna like this was the end of everything. We had done this before, we were well practised in goodbye hugs.

As they led me away I heard Jenna shout at Demelza, 'What did you mean when you said you knew things?' But her shout was choked with tears. I didn't hear any reply.

What could anyone know about Zach that wasn't bad? Could anything get us out of this mess?

3

BATTLE LINES

Leaving Jenna felt unreal, but none of this was close to real life. A teenage army, Zach in charge, surely this couldn't happen? I had to find the key to changing it all. What had Miss Tregarthur done?

After I had been dragged off from our prison cell, I was shoved into the back of an old army truck. Old as in old for me, probably newer for the people driving it. But it wasn't long before I joined a well organised movement of soldiers being sent to the front of this war. We pulled up outside a building that looked like a school, but with no one around, then the bus arrived. Another old vehicle, but this one looked well used, mud stained, scratches along the sides, a faded advert on the back for something called Nestlé's Milk and a picture of a soldier. The soldier looked older; did they only exist in pictures?

I was loaded into the bus with people my age and younger, teenagers, but all dressed in army uniforms. Some had old and dirty kit, others like me seemed new to this. The old uniforms were a mess, stained with what had to be blood. Blood that was all male and young. Even I knew that teenagers had always joined armies, kids in wars around the world, but here they were in charge. There were no old soldiers in this army.

We joined other groups being herded onto a convoy of old buses and we moved from place to place, picking up more people. Looking out I saw that the fields were being worked entirely by women – girls, as young as Jenna. Some older women, but no men. Whatever was happening it hadn't changed the old male and female roles on fighting. Jenna was going to love that, my only hope at the moment was that she would start a revolution.

Wherever we were going on this bus journey it gave me too much time to think, and Miss Tregarthur filled those thoughts. I had thought she was finished. The last we saw of her was when she was being dragged into the very stones of Dartmoor. Dragged in and screaming while a storm crashed around us. She had been taken into the moor and if that old man was right, Miss Tregarthur had become the spirit in the time tunnel, or whatever it was that transported us through time. But she wasn't just a tunnel, she had changed time. The only way we could get out of this mess was to stop her, and me going to war wasn't going to do that. There didn't look like any escape.

Some of the soldiers were in charge, sort of guards.

'Anyone thinking of running off?' said one of them. 'Running gets you shot and we like the practice.' He laughed and pointed his gun at us. The guards were the only ones with guns. When were we going to get our guns? That might be the time to escape.

The journey went on and on.

We changed buses in a small town. That's when I saw the first older men, they were all injured. Some were on crutches and one man, in a wheel chair, was holding a clipboard and organising the transport. He gave us all numbers and said we had to remember them. I didn't even try. The man in the wheel chair might be older, but only just. There really weren't any very old people. I tried to ask the others what was happening, as we were moved from place to place, but they didn't answer. Bleak blank faces stared back at me, looking at me as though I was an idiot.

'What does it matter?' one boy replied when I asked him yet again about the war. 'You'll soon find out. But it won't be for long. None of us will live for long.' He turned his head to the window, resting his forehead on the glass, and I saw his chest heave.

It was on the third, or was it the fourth, bus that I saw Jack. Sitting halfway down the coach, by the window but sprawled over the seat, making it clear that he didn't want company. Did he recognise me?

'Jack,' I shouted.

He snapped upright with the blankest of faces, shaking his head when he saw me.

'Do I know you?' His head fell back and it didn't look as though he wanted an answer. It didn't look as though he cared who I was. Perhaps he could see I wasn't important enough to cause him trouble.

Jack was one of the people who had come on the first walk, right at the beginning of this mess, before Miss Tregarthur had moved us about in time. Jack, Mary and the others, on a school hike across the moor which ended up in a time of mammoths and sabre tooth tigers. And there was worse, we had moved on to the Black Death and it wasn't just the plague, the villagers planned to see us burn to death.

But I'd thought that Jack and Mary had escaped back home. We'd parted in the time tunnel; the crowd of villagers screaming at us, ready to start their fire.

I couldn't leave Jack. I made my way down the bus towards him, pushed his stuff aside and sat in the empty seat beside him. It was only the new recruits that sat together. The others all sat alone, not speaking.

'Jack?'

He said nothing and shook his head. I put my hand on his shoulder.

'Leave me alone.' He shook my hand away.

'It's me, Alvin. Don't you remember? Where's Mary?'

Jack slumped forward, covering his eyes with his hands. 'Why do you have to do this? Can't you just go back to your seat?'

'No,' I said. 'Where's Mary?' I repeated.

Jack's eyes blazed. 'Don't talk to me about Mary. Why do you talk about her? I'll never see her again. We're all going to die.'

That was too much. I turned in the seat, grabbed his shoulders and shook him hard. 'Jack, get a grip. It's me, Alvin. This is all Miss Tregarthur. It isn't real. She's done this, we have to find a way out.'

Jack stared into my eyes. 'There is no way out, don't you understand. We're going to the war. You don't escape the war. Nobody escapes the war.'

The bus went on. Travelling was cramped and uncomfortable, as was trying to get Jack to say anything. I heard other people talking about crossing the sea to France. Someone said we might not make it, German warships or submarines would sink us. Someone else said we had airships flying overhead to spot the submarines.

'That's just a myth, there aren't any airships,' Jack muttered. I hoped he might say a bit more.

'Why don't they use jets and helicopters? That's what chased us off the moor. Chased us and fired at the cavemen?' I said, and that seemed to spark some memory.

'They're just American,' Jack snarled. 'Bloody Americans.'

But that did start him off. This war was only happening in the place we were going to.

'Some countries stopped the fighting in other parts of the world,' Jack explained. 'Just so long as they stick to the rules.'

'Rules?'

'Yep, rules.' Jack gave a miserable laugh. 'The other countries agreed not to get involved, just to let us carry on the fighting with the Germans.'

The Americans and Russians had modern aeroplanes and they weren't allowed to use them in the war. But it seemed that the Americans had taken an interest in the cavemen. Jack didn't have any idea why the Americans would fly their jets against them.

'But there's always stuff going on that we don't understand,' Jack said, looking around, and I could see he was worried that the rest of the bus seemed to be listening.

'But Zach?' I said.

'Shh, you have to say, "Supreme Commander", you can get into trouble using his name without permission.'

'Supreme what? Who cares about Zach?'

'You'll care. If you do anything they don't like ...' Jack didn't seem to want to tell me about anything that could be worse than the mess we were in right now.

'Who are the "they"?' I looked around the bus, there didn't

seem to be anyone in charge. But then I looked again at the front. Sitting next to the driver was someone in a different uniform. For a start it was cleaner, but it had a red collar, there were red stripes down the sides of his trousers, and he had a red cap. 'Is he one of them? The red boy?'

I pointed. Jack grabbed my arm and pulled it down.

The red soldier turned, 'Keep it down, or you know what will happen,' he said and it would have been scary except the soldier was probably about fourteen and his voice squeaked. I found it hard not to laugh.

'You have to be careful,' Jack spoke a bit more in whispers, looking to see if the guard turned around. 'If you get to be a guard it's better, they say you don't have to fight. But only if they hand out punishments. The more punishments, the longer they are allowed to stay away from the war. I'm pretty sure they still end up fighting and being killed in the end.'

Slowly I managed to get Jack to tell me a bit more. He didn't know how long this war had been going on.

'Some people say it's 1917 in this part of Europe,' Jack said. 'That could be true. Fits with the war, I suppose. If it is 1917 then it's been that year for ages, always 1917.'

'But they didn't have helicopters and jets in 1917,' I mumbled, not making any sense of this.

'The rest of the world seems to have moved on. Here it is always something like 1917. We're in a never-ending war. Each year the same happens. It's not going to stop until everyone is dead. There's nothing to stop it. Each side has pretty much the same weapons.' That made me think of another time. When we had seen plans for tanks and guns.

When there had been talk of spies. Did this have anything to do with the man called Masterson? A man we'd met in a different time. He'd been a spy. I'd hoped we had messed up his plans, maybe we hadn't.

'But why do you all keep going out to this war?' I asked. 'I mean if you're all going to get killed, why bother, why not attack these red guards, there are a lot of us on this bus, we could do it.'

'We just do it, we just go to the war, I suppose,' Jack stared at me. 'There's something that keeps us in this cycle that keeps this war going on and on.'

'That has to be something Miss Tregarthur has done,' I stared back at him. 'We've got to stop her.'

Jack snorted a laugh, 'No chance. Now we are down to only teenage soldiers. When we're all dead I suppose it might stop.' Jack poked the window, we were passing graveyards; white crosses for miles and miles and we were still in England. 'You're in what's left of the 6th Brigade,' Jack pointed to a badge on my shoulder. I hadn't noticed it before.

'Where exactly are we going?' I asked.

'It's called the Somme,' Jack replied in a deep, whispered, voice as though I'd know what that meant. I did, even I had heard of the Battle of the Somme. That stopped me asking questions but not wondering how we were going to get out of this.

Looking around me, the weird thing was that this bus wasn't filled with terrified kids. They all seemed to have accepted that this was the way it was, as though it was normal. They were expecting it, going to war was what happened. Even the ones returning, sitting alone with blank pale faces, they were still going back. Somehow, Miss Tregarthur's time mess had made this nightmare into a bizarre normality. There was to be no way out for any of us.

In silence, we turned through a gate into a muddy sort of car park with rows of old coaches and hundreds of soldiers. It looked like some sort of old car rally to me, dirty cream coloured buses all with adverts on the back – milk, Bovril, and adverts to persuade you to join up. That seemed odd; there wasn't a choice about joining this war.

Pouring out of these buses came a mixture of new and returning soldiers. Again, all those who had been before stood, heads hanging and silent. Amongst the new recruits the occasional shoving, pushing and messing about – sort of what you would expect from a teenage army, and we hadn't got any guns yet. The red-suits marched in and started competing for brutality awards.

'You,' one of them pointed to a plump boy. 'Come here.'

This was obviously well practised. The boy sniggered to others around him and shuffled his way towards the band of guards.

'Didn't we tell you to shut up?' the guard said.

'No,' the boy said.

The guards set on him, using the wooden butts of their guns – old guns – to smash into his stomach and force him, blubbering, to the ground. It worked. We all shut up. They boy crawled back to his group.

I might have been ready to do something, but Jack held me back, 'They always do this. If you try to stop them, they'll kill someone – probably you.' I did nothing.

We were marched down a pier and onto a boat. Some boat. It must have once been a cruise liner, taking tourists somewhere on holiday. A big rusty ship with steam coming from two funnels. I could see a huge tear in the railing above me as we approached.

'Shell damage,' Jack whispered.

Before the war, if there had been a 'before', you could imagine normal families having holidays on this ship, children running along the decks, people having fun. No fun here this time. The ship was a near wreck, it had been splashed with green and brown paint in some pretty useless attempt at camouflage, didn't really need it because the dirty rust seemed to meld in with everything around.

'Nothing gets repaired,' Jack muttered. 'No one knows how to repair things. The captain's some old bloke who got injured.'

'How old?'

'About twenty, I think.'

The boat steamed out from the jetty and soon we were in the open sea. We'd been hustled up to the top deck and outside. Pushed up stairways, once they must have been carpeted, you could see the remains, ripped up by the boots of soldiers, decorations broken, pictures on the walls smashed. And the smell. There was a smell of something very bad as we went through the boat. The decks outside were crammed with soldiers. The sea was rough and soon the deck became slippery as sea-sickness took over, including mine. Even if you threw up over the side, the wind blew most of it back.

A group of red guards pushed through, shouting, 'Keep watching the sea, watch out for German boats, watch out if you want to live.'

Jack said it wasn't worth looking out, 'Nothing you can do. They're meant to have guns on this boat, but if they do, then they don't work. Nothing works this far from the front line, and even there most things are broken.'

It started to rain. It felt like hours of a wet, rough, dangerous passage across to France. At least the rain washed the vomit away. There was almost no cover for anyone – except for the red guards who were the only ones allowed to shelter.

'Why don't you let us go below, this boat must have loads of cabins?' I asked a red guard who had run to throw up over the side of the boat.

'Ask him,' the guard pushed past me and pointed to another of the soldiers returning to the war; a veteran.

'No one goes down to the cabins,' the soldier squeaked and tried to get his breaking voice under control. 'They say the cabins are full of dead bodies waiting to be buried.' I didn't think he could be older than twelve.

What he said matched the smell. But why?

'Why don't they throw the bodies overboard?' I couldn't understand why this boat was going back and forward across the sea and still carrying dead bodies.

'It's an order,' Jack said as the squeaky soldier left us. Jack went on: 'There are lots of orders that seem to stick. I guess someone must have made the order that the bodies stayed on this ship until they could be buried. Probably whoever made that order is dead, but no one has thought to make a new order or to bury the bodies. You find lots of orders like that, it's the way the war is run.'

The boat gave another lurch as it crossed a huge wave. I clung on, trying not to puke and watching the grey sea foaming around the ship as we rumbled towards the dark line of land ahead.

The ship slowed as we reached a pile of wrecked army vehicles, heaped up in the sea, a sort of jetty. As we neared I could see they were all old rusting ancient trucks, the sort I'd seen in pictures, but those had been ancient pictures used to tell us about the war that had once ended, not like this one that still went on. We bumped and scraped into the jetty. There were a few giant things like balloons which were meant to keep us away from the sides, but not enough. Each crash knocked us over as we made our way forward on the deck.

We had to scramble down rope ladders thrown from the side of the boat. In the wind and rain, it was difficult and dangerous. I was glad of the time I had once spent on sailing boats. Not everyone made it to shore without falling into the sea. Not all those who fell in could swim. You could still hear the screams, even above all the other noises.

'Move it,' someone shouted over and over: 'Germans,' as we heard a shell scream over us and explode. Another followed, closer this time, we scrambled as fast as we could. No one helped the people in the sea.

On shore, we ran towards the dunes at the back of the beach. More shells fell near the ship, which set off and was soon hidden in murky mist and rain.

Looking over the top of the dunes, this was somewhere from hell. We couldn't be far from the front line here. Mud and craters all around, destroyed army vehicles, houses with too few walls, horses stumbling along rutted roads, men being marched off with their faces showing total confusion. This was a place of confusion – confusion and I couldn't see any hope of escape.

We were still being moved, with shouts from the guards.

Soon we reached a rail track and the remains of a station - just a concrete platform. This wasn't a passenger train, just a long row of wagons, the sort of thing that might be used for cows or other animals. We were herded on board.

'They've been using these trains for years to get people to the front. Steam trains,' Jack helped me to climb up. 'You've got to get to the side of the wagon and sit on the floor, otherwise you fall about when we hit something.'

'The train hits things? What things?' I did what he said and we sat jamming our backs against the wood of the ancient railway carriage. The carriage filled to a cramped sweatiness and the door was slammed shut, and, I think, bolted.

'Bodies.' Jack turned away. 'Bodies on the line, that's what we hit. Might be yours soon.'

'Bodies, here? Are the Germans here? Is the fighting here?' I worried that we might all get killed in the dark - there weren't any windows – killed before we even got to the front.

'Not really, the guns do drop shells and we may get blown up, but all the fighting is in the trenches, you'll soon see that,' Jack gave another half laugh. Listening to him and the others it seemed as though they were all trying to pretend to be brave while expecting death at any minute.

'So, what bodies are there here?'

'Runners,' Jack said. 'If you try to run then it's impossible not to use the railway lines, no roads are passable, they just wait and shoot you if you run. That's where the bodies come from, fallen on the line.'

And just as he said that there was a thump from under the train, a lurch as the carriages swung crazily before settling back to the normal rumble.

'Train clears them out of the way and they don't bury these bodies,' Jack's grim voice sounded nothing like the boy I knew from school. 'That's probably why there aren't any windows. No one wants you to see how many have tried to run from the war. No one gets away. The red guards get extra points for shooting deserters.'

That shut me up, but there had to be something I could do. This was all Miss Tregarthur's doing, and she was killing thousands, millions, and it wouldn't stop until there was no one left to carry a gun. How old would a soldier be who couldn't carry a gun? I wondered, and I didn't have to ask.

'When there aren't enough to fight then the other side are going to come over and kill everyone left. That's what the guards say, that's when they say we have to keep fighting or the enemy will kill all the women back in England. That's what they say, that's what …' Jack lowered his voice, 'what High Commander Zach says when he comes on his visits to the trenches.'

To me that sounded more like an opportunity than a threat. If Zach came out here then there had to be some chance of stopping this. When do they give us the guns, I wondered?

'Don't bother to think of shooting him,' Jack had obviously read my thoughts. 'We have to hand in all the guns when he comes. Too many have thought about shooting our Great Commander.'

They gave us the guns when we climbed down from the rail trucks. Racks of rifles that looked old even here. Someone might have tried to clean them once but it would have been useless. It wasn't just the dirt, most of them were damaged. You just had to take what you were given.

-4-

MUD AND MORE MUD

It was everywhere. Mud. I'd seen old black and white pictures of this war. The terrible First World War; but just a war between Britain and the Germans? And just in one place? Surely there had been more people and countries in this fight? What had happened to the other people in Europe? There wasn't much point in asking because nobody seemed to know anything, especially about food, and I was hungry.

Bread arrived. It came in long loaves, trays of them being passed along the line. I thought they were French, they looked French. So maybe there were French people fighting somewhere – or maybe they had agreed to bake bread and that kept them out of the fighting now.

But even those old photos couldn't tell the story of what this was like. I'd seen pictures of men lining up in deep trenches, men getting ready to leap up and fight the enemy, sandbag huts and even pictures of the dead. That must have happened years ago in this cycle of war. Everything had been left and nothing repaired or changed.

The weather and fighting had rampaged over this battle field. The trenches ran with water, two or three feet deep in places, pulling down the muddy sides. The water ran foul, there were no latrines anywhere that hadn't been clogged up, and you didn't leave the trench because you got shot. Oh yes, the fighting was still going on, bullets whizzing overhead. When I peeked out during a quiet time I could see the battle field in front of us, and the other side not much more than a few hundred yards away. And the dead. Dead soldiers' bodies spread across the ground broken by the guns and shells. Between them the wrecked remains of army vehicles, rusting and dripping with water, tangled in barb wire. A stage set for a zombie movie could not have been worse, or smelt worse.

'It gets better after a day or two,' Jack was talking about the smell.

'Completely better when you get killed. Can't smell a thing when you're dead,' someone called out.

Bread came with bullets. Piles of bullets ready to be loaded into these ancient guns. The guns were dangerous. 'Don't shoot them unless you really have to,' Jack said. 'They often explode when you fire them.'

'When do you really have to use them?' I was wondering how dangerous my gun was.

'You'll know,' Jack looked away.

I guess he meant when someone else was about to shoot you. It seemed more likely we would get killed by our own guns rather than the enemy. We didn't know how to keep them clean. This teenage army was running very short of any knowledge. Machine guns stood uselessly pointing at the sky. Occasionally a shell would launch from the other side and crash into soldier groups, splattering more bodies into the air. Shells didn't come often, we seemed to fire even fewer back at them. The war was settling into hand to hand combat only.

Because this was a cycle, the year was being fought over and over again with the same orders. July 4th was coming up again. Any soldier who had been here for more than a year knew what that meant – we would be sent over the top. And it seemed like just as many were killed each year, just younger. Dead and hopeless, forced back by the other side. And on July 5th the enemy did the same. Out they came from their own stinking trench, blazing away, their guns just as self-exploding, before we would shoot them in hundreds.

And Miss Tregarthur had managed another cruel trick. As we prepared for the 4th we were joined by other soldiers – Matt, Stevie, and Ryan. I knew them all. They had come out on the first walk. The school expedition that had started this whole mess in time. Big Matt was the same – big and a bit slow, Stevie was the boy who used to whine, this time he said nothing and stared blankly in a crazy sort of way. Ryan said little and shifted from foot to foot as though he was expecting something to arrive, and not something good.

None of them had a clear idea of who I was or what I was talking about. They didn't exactly say I was making it up. They seemed to remember a few things. Nothing about school. But that had to be a time thing, we were years from our own real time. Did that mean that none of the things had happened to them, even if the actual things had happened so long in the past? But where had this lot come from? That sort of question just didn't work, they came from here, obviously, and when I asked how, well, it all became a bit silly.

Stevie said very little. In fact, he didn't say anything unless you asked questions. Then he seemed to jump to attention.

He seemed like someone waiting to be hurt. Eventually he told us that he'd been sent out two years before, I guess someone had got fed up with him and sent him here even though he was younger than the age for fighting, which seemed to have slipped down a couple more years.

Stevie had been sent out on reconnaissance, that meant crawling through rain filled trenches that had been abandoned, trenches that went forward towards the German position. He'd been told to listen in on the enemy. But he'd been blasted by the noise of explosions – no one had told him that was going to happen. He'd managed to get a signal back from one of the enemy, identifying a nest of soldiers sheltering from whatever weather was being thrown at them. The message meant that shells could be fired. It didn't seem to matter that Stevie was still there. He didn't whine or use many words. He just stared out into whatever. Occasionally he'd try to jump up and leave the trench. Matt told me that Stevie wanted to die, he couldn't stand the life here. Matt's job was to keep Stevie alive, even if Stevie didn't like the idea.

Ryan had once been a friend of Zach's – most of the time. But Zach didn't treat his friends well. Ryan had escaped Zach's plan to have him killed by a sabre tooth tiger. He didn't think he was going to escape dying in this war.

We tried to clean our guns, tried to get ready for the next day – July 4th. Jack told me that in the beginning the soldiers used to write letters before they went over the top to fight.

'Don't do that now, it just upsets anyone left at home,' Jack sniffed a sob. 'They know we'll die soon enough.'

'They don't let the women fight then?' I asked.

'Not allowed,' Jack explained. 'It's some world agreement

thing with the other nations, neither side is allowed to use women in the trenches. Someone said they were too weak.'

I hoped they didn't tell Jenna about that. But for once I could see the benefit of inequality. Perhaps I should have stayed in the dress I'd worn back in the time when we escaped from prison. Would I have escaped this war? That made me think of Sam and Ivy and of course the baby. At least they were in Australia and would hopefully avoid the war – but they were in a different age – a hundred years ago. Not the same war then?

I'd seen it on the telly, knew what we would have to do, scramble out and run towards the machine guns.

I heard one young soldier say under his breath: 'Try to keep someone in front of you.'

But if you did that, everyone slowed and was mowed down. I was going to lead, had to lead. That had happened on the very first trip in time; everyone followed me. I had no idea why. Back in the misty bits of school days it certainly would not have happened. I was not the sort of person to follow, unless you were really into danger. My family specialised in danger. Everything changed for me when we set out on that hike those – what was it - years ago?

The first time we set out on with Miss Tregarthur it had been around this time of year. End of the summer term. Back in that time, I'd been sent to my aunt and uncle, but they'd decided I was old enough to be thrown out when I got to sixteen. I was getting ready for time on the streets, nowhere else to go. Was that years ago, or years ahead? Time travel is impossible to understand.

Strange how those thoughts of home and school filled my mind as we waited for the whistle. I suppose it was because I didn't expect to be alive at the end of this day.

The whistle blew, the signal for 'go' and we went. Jack, Matt, Stevie, and Ryan charging with me. We made about fifty yards. Soldiers were falling all around us. These weren't brave men, just kids screaming as they went down, some shot, some terrified. There was no organisation, no older officers to take charge, it was like a kid's game except for being lethal. I couldn't see any point in going on, there was only death ahead. Jack stumbled and I fell into him as we all tumbled into a huge shell hole and the others followed.

This must have been the worst place in the world. Half full of water and the other half of dead bodies. The day was warming up and so was the smell.

'We have to go on,' Jack moaned. 'If we don't then we get shot when we get back.'

'Eh?' I grunted.

'They'll say its cowardice and you always get shot for cowardice.'

I didn't think it made much difference who you got shot by, but Jack was trying to get us to leave the shell-hole. I looked around, Ryan wasn't there.

'Wait,' shouted Stevie. 'Look.'

Stevie was pointing at a gap in the side of this stinking hole. Matt pulled several bodies out of the way.

'It's one of the tunnels they sent me down,' Stevie shuddered. We waited for him to say more, it was quite difficult to hear over the gun-fire and the Germans were firing shells that exploded near us.

Jack was getting frantic. Apparently, the shells often exploded in the same place, because the Germans didn't move the guns.

'In here,' Stevie called again and he half crawled and half slid into the opening. 'Leave the rifles,' Stevie shouted back. 'They aren't any use.'

We left them.

I had no idea if this opening led anywhere but I could see why Stevie had been picked. They used the youngest and smallest to go forward and spy on the other side. There was only just enough space for me to follow Stevie. I heard Matt grunting as he squashed in behind me. Jack was somewhere at the back.

It was almost completely dark but there seemed to be a way forward. In places shafts of light came through holes that might have been made by shells. But we were definitely in a tunnel. I hit my elbow on a piece of wood that seemed to have been placed to keep the roof from collapsing.

We were scrabbling forward on our stomachs. I wasn't sure why we were in here, if a shell landed directly above us then we were all dead – buried alive. And I couldn't see how we could go back, there wasn't room to turn. But we went on, following Stevie. Something in the way he led made me feel this was a good choice. Actually, probably the only choice if we were to have any chance of living.

We could hear the battle going on above as we shuffled forward. Stevie was ahead and kept stopping, 'Come on, it should open at the end.' I didn't ask him what we would find at the end. If this was a spy tunnel, then it would probably take us behind the enemy lines. That just meant we'd be shot by a different bullet.

We were into sticky mud and could not see any more shafts of light. Something scrabbled passed me. A rat, I thought. If the tunnel got any narrower then there would be no hope at all, just exhausted death in the dark. I thought of Jenna. Hoped she would survive. Then we heard voices.

'Shh,' hissed Stevie, and he disappeared in front of me.

Crawling on I felt the ground disappear in front of me. I couldn't raise my head enough to see what was happening but we seemed to arrive in a bigger mud space.

'Was this another cave?' I groaned to myself. We'd always found caves across time and they nearly always meant danger, but at least here was some space.

The four of us crammed into the underground cave. We could hear the voices more clearly. Stevie kept on whispering for us to shut up. He pointed up at a dim glow of light. I could just see a small hole in the mud to one side of us. I felt Stevie squirming, searching before he reached out and stuffed something into the hole.

'I stuffed it with an old jacket. It stops them hearing us,' Stevie still whispered. 'That hole must go through to the Germans.' I could only just hear his words. 'This is the sort of place I had to sit in for ages, hoping to get useful information. That's how I knew I'd find something to shove in the hole. Something we always left behind.'

'Listen.' He pulled out the jacket.

We listened. My only German stretched to 'achtung' but of course, Stevie was fluent. That's why they'd used him. I had no idea where he'd picked that up. I would have to remember to ask him when we got back. That made me snort and get a prod from Stevie to keep quiet. There was no point in thinking about returning. Even if we crawled all the way back we'd probably get shot for not fighting.

'No sound, listen,' Stevie gave us another hurried whisper. I suppose he didn't know we couldn't understand. There were two voices, and I heard a definite 'achtung' as one of them dropped something.

'Explosives,' Stevie leaned over to me and leant so close his muddy nose poked me in the eye. A little later the voices stopped.

'I think they've gone,' I said when we'd heard no sounds for several minutes.

'They've made a pile of explosives,' Stevie explained. 'They're planning to put a machine gun on top, not one that works, but something to make our troops go for it, then they'll blow them all up.'

To me, it sounded like a good plan. Except we were just feet away from this pile of explosives. But then a sort of an idea came to me. I poked my hand into the listening hole. I could just reach to the end. It felt as though it had been blocked with something, I guessed to try and hide it. I pushed and I think it must have been a stone because I heard it drop against something. Explosives, I hoped.

'We need to blow this up before any of our lot try to make for the machine gun,' I said into the darkness. 'Any ideas?'

'We could use this.' Jack scrabbled in his jacket and held something up to me. In the gloomy dark I had no idea what he was holding.

'It's a grenade, new type, I nicked it before coming out this time,' Jack said. 'Someone told me it could save your life. You just pull out this string, lob it and it explodes a few seconds later.'

'What, so we blow up this pile of explosives a few feet away?' I muttered at him.

'It's what you're meant to do in war,' Matt spoke for almost the first time. 'Die, to save others.'

I wasn't keen on the idea.

'Have to get a move on,' Stevie said. 'The battle is getting closer.' And the gunfire was definitely louder now.

Jack had always been good at coming up with new ideas. Jack and Mary had saved us many times before. And Jack had a plan.

'I need your boot laces,' Jack said firmly and we didn't ask why but bent awkwardly to pull them out of our boots.

'I'm going to tie them to the string on the grenade.' Jack took the laces. 'Alvin, you've got the longest arms, you push the grenade through the hole. Then we get back in the tunnel, I pull the string and BANG.'

I thought there were a pile of problems with this, not the least that the string might just set the grenade off when it dropped on the other side. But at least it was something to do, if we waited we were going to get blown up anyway. So we did it. Pushed the grenade through the hole and slowly felt it drop. Jack wanted to be the last and pull the rope of laces, but I pushed him into the tunnel. Stevie led the way again, Matt and Jack followed. I crawled after them. I hadn't gone far before I felt the string of bootlaces tighten.

'Ready?' I shouted and pulled as we all crawled as fast as we could.

5

A MEDAL FOR JACK

The explosion hit, everything suddenly so bright, a hard wave of sound smashing into me. I thought my head was going to fall off; there was a screaming pain in my ears and I felt a razor hot bolt shoot up my leg. I must have passed out, but not for long, I came round in a rain of mud.

The explosion lifted the mud high in the air, mud from above the explosives, and from a blast that shot along our tunnel, blowing off the roof. We were in the open as the mud rain fell on us.

Jack had been in front. He turned to me, shouting, but I could hear nothing. He mouthed, 'Run, run.' I tried to get up.

I'm sure he was right, we were probably behind enemy lines. It wouldn't be long before they found us. Jack turned to run, pulling Stevie with him. I fell back, not moving. Looking down I could see the bloody wound below my knee. Somehow it didn't hurt, in the silence it felt as though everything had finished. There was no war because I could hear no guns, I couldn't hear anything at all.

I felt Matt pick me up. He did it on his own. So much stronger. I thought back to the first day when Matt and I had helped to save someone trapped by falling rocks, fleeing from Miss Tregarthur's earthquake. A simple school hike that had sent us back thousands of years into a time of cavemen and mammoths.

That image and every one of the weird things we had seen seemed to come into my mind as Matt ran, half dragging me, stumbling through shell holes, tripping over dead soldiers. Sound was coming back to me along with pain. I tried to cry out as Matt dumped me back in our own trenches. I heard the guns firing again, a constant blast from the other side. We had wrecked the enemy plans. But were the Germans our enemy or just Miss Tregarthur? That was my last thought before a wave of blackness seemed to sweep over my body and I lost consciousness.

'Ryan,' I shouted, I had to find Ryan. Where had he got to? I felt someone holding me down. 'I have to find Ryan,' I was screaming his name. Slowly things cleared. Matt and Jack were holding me down. I was on the floor in some makeshift first aid part of the trench. I winced in pain from my leg. 'Where's Ryan?' I shouted, confused, why was I so worried about Ryan?

But I was worried. I didn't remember seeing or hearing from him when we set the grenade.

'He didn't come,' Jack said, still holding on to me. 'He didn't follow us in the tunnel, he stayed behind. He never made it over the top. They…'

Jack stopped.

'Tell me.' I grabbed his arm.

'They shot him, said he didn't fight, said he was a coward,' Jack choked.

When had that happened? I couldn't remember. 'How long have I been out?'

'Maybe a day,' Jack replied. 'Difficult to follow time here.'

That got to me. Another dead person. Miss Tregarthur again. Was it my fault? She was after me. Had I done something that made her start all this killing, when she really just wanted me dead? I couldn't understand why our own side had killed Ryan. He wasn't the greatest person in the world, but he wasn't that bad. He'd been through so much. He'd saved himself from being killed by Zach or killed by a sabre tooth tiger back in the time of the cavemen. But he'd been shot by someone who should have been helping him. No wonder the war went on and on, it had made animals of these soldiers. Wilder than any tiger and more dangerous. But they weren't soldiers, just kids caught up in Miss Tregarthur's terrible legacy. She might be buried in the rocks of Dartmoor but somehow her foul mind had brought about this terrible carnage that wouldn't stop.

I looked down at my bandaged leg. Blood was still seeping through. I saw Stevie, his arm was bandaged but he still managed a nod. I suppose he wanted to show that he was at least still alive.

At that moment, a smartly dressed soldier came to the door. 'Well done lads,' he said. That nearly made me laugh. I thought he looked as though he'd learnt how to be an officer by watching an old film. His voice sounded like some old newsreader. Or it would have done if this officer hadn't been about fifteen.

'There'll be a medal for you, soldier,' he said to Jack. 'Good show. And one for your chums.' And that did make me laugh even though it hurt, in fact my whole body hurt. I wondered how much of me had been injured.

Another soldier with red crosses on his uniform came in, took my arm and jabbed me with a syringe before he left without saying anything. The world started swimming again.

When I came round again I was in the open air. Moving my head, I could see my bandaged leg. Stevie along with Matt and Jack were sitting a little way off. It turned out that we were going to avoid fighting for a while – Stevie and me because we were injured. Jack and Matt because they were waiting for medals. There was going to be a medal ceremony. It took me a while before I sorted all that out. I managed to avoid being given another jab of whatever knocked me out. It seemed that apart from bruises, my leg was the only seriously damaged bit of me. That along with some blast damage which meant I couldn't hear too well.

'Who's presenting the medals?' I asked, probably the next day, when things seemed calmer.

'Who do you think?' Jack spat out his words. 'Zach, of course. He's coming to inspect the troops, they always have the Supreme Commander after this battle.'

'Was that a battle? I thought the fighting went on all the time,' I said.

'It does, but this one was special. Apparently when the war first started this was the day they captured a wood,' Jack didn't sound too happy about this. 'It was a day that thousands died and they've kept on doing the same thing every year, on and on.'

That stopped us talking for a while. I started thinking of Zach. If he was coming here then it meant there was a chance of getting at him. I needed another of Jack's grenades. If I could kill Zach maybe there would be a chance to end the war.

'When's he coming?' I asked.

'Tomorrow, I guess.' Jack pointed to a group of soldiers who seemed to be building a platform. 'Zach will stand up there and we go up for our medals. Me, Matt and Stevie. You'll be paraded in a wheelchair, if they can find one.'

Matt turned away. None of us cared about medals, but I cared about Zach.

'What's that?' I saw a group who were spraying clouds of white powder around the platform.

'No idea,' said Jack. 'Always happens when Zach turns up at the front. It's some sort of poison, they say.'

We watched the platform being built. I wanted to think of a way to get at Zach, but the pain in my leg made that difficult. Matt asked if he could do anything to help.

'Thanks for saving my life,' I said to him.

'You may not thank me when they send you back to fight. That's if your leg recovers.'

I seemed to remember wounds didn't recover too well in the war when they didn't have any antibiotics. I'm sure that was something we talked about in that time when we saved the King of England from the Black Death – saved him because Mary had a packet of pills to treat acne. Turned out they were just the thing we needed then and we needed them now.

'Jack, come here for minute.' I quietly explained to him my idea for killing Zach.

'No chance,' Jack said loudly enough for the other two to hear. 'Everyone's thought of murdering him. That's why they search you before you go up to get a medal. Too many soldiers want him dead and he knows it. He just likes to strut up there along with his new girlfriend. She comes with him.'

'At least that'll upset Demelza,' I said and we all laughed. It seemed that in this mess of death and fighting, the smallest thing could make you laugh. Strange what it did to us.

The next day there was a band. It wasn't a great band. Ok, they had all the instruments but it seemed that 'When the saints go marching in' was the only tune they had a vague chance of playing. And they marched. This was the marching band of the Supreme Commander. Jack told me they always played when he came to inspect the troops, which wasn't very often. They played then his men searched anyone who was going to come within a mile of him. After the search, Zach would climb up on the stage, say how wonderful his army was, give out the medals and then run for it.

Except he didn't. He didn't do any of that. Because the search didn't take place and it wasn't him that took to the stage. It wasn't him that told the troops that it was really hoped that the war could be ended soon and it wasn't Zach who called for Jack and Matt, and actually me and Stevie as well. It wasn't Zach dressed in some super-smart army uniform. It was Jenna who stood before the troops and they cheered. Jenna and Demelza, where had they come from? If this was a dream, it suddenly got better, unless it was my injury making me hallucinate.

We left the war on the day after Jack had got his medal, headed for England. I think it was the best day of my life. The only bit that wasn't so great was that Demelza was still with us, but I had to accept it had been Demelza who got us out of the mess. She hadn't stopped the war, she'd just stopped Zach.

'Rats,' Demelza said, with a smirk. But all this was going to take a lot more explanation.

6

BLIND PANIC

After the medal ceremony Jenna – or Field Marshall Karen – led us to her staff car.

'What? How?' I stuttered as I limped over to the large vehicle. They hadn't found a wheelchair.

'What, how, *Ma'am*.' Jenna had to hide her smile. 'That's what you have to say.'

I might call Jenna by her new title but I wasn't calling Demelza an admiral or whatever she had dreamt herself up to be.

Demelza was looking really pleased with herself. 'Like the car?' she grinned. The car was a great big American wagon with space in the back for all of us. Not the regular old British things that littered the battle field. A big comfortable wagon. The sort of wagon I might have seen back in my own time. What was going on?

Jenna pointed to the soldier in the driving seat and placed her finger over her lips, 'Later.'

'Good to see you, ma'am,' Jack said in professional soldier manner and saluted. That almost made Jenna fall over, coughing to hide her laughter.

I climbed into the car. This was unbelievable, but behind me the sounds of the war were still going on, teenagers being shot, blown up, dying of disease. We still had to find a way to make things right, a way to stop Miss Tregarthur, why had she done this? Was it just to get rid of me? Maybe there was nothing else she could do, buried in the stones of Dartmoor with just hate and anger to drive her on. I was stuck with those thoughts as we drove back to the coast.

'Wow,' we all said looking at a fast, new boat tied to the makeshift dock. Jenna and Demelza led the way. Loads of soldiers lined up to make more salutes as we boarded. We took off fast, I guess the captain didn't want to stay around. We could still hear the sound of shells being fired.

'What about submarines?' Jack asked, looking out over the water.

'Radar,' Demelza whispered. Neither of them were going to give us any explanation until we were alone.

I'd been given a space to sit with my leg up. The pain and throbbing seemed to get worse as we went over the waves. My body was damp with a clammy sweat, I guessed the wound was infected. In this age, it probably meant I'd lose the leg – or die. Miss Tregarthur would like that.

Jenna looked at me and frowned and said something to Demelza who called one of the soldiers, actually they were sailors and in blue uniforms – must be the navy.

'Radio on to get an ambulance and have the hospital on stand-by,' Demelza ordered. I suppose with her being an Admiral, or something, she was in charge of the navy here. Last time I'd seen Jenna and Demelza they were going to be sent off to a farm, working to produce food for the war effort. Here they seemed to be in charge of everything. What had happened to Zach? My head was swimming. Was it just this mess of thoughts that made it swim, but I wasn't seeing too clearly. Slowly I felt myself slide off the seat. I wasn't going to find out anything for a while.

Home. I had to be back in my own time. A hospital, a small ward. I was the only patient. Two or three other empty beds. Above me a drip held a pack of blood running down to my arm, on my left was a thing that kept beeping with a trace which just had to be my heart rate. There was even a bowl of grapes on the locker next to me. I was alive and back home. There was no Miss Tregarthur, no war, and no mess of time to escape.

Jack looked up from the chair on my other side, 'Hi.' He was wearing an army uniform. It wasn't over. Nothing had changed. The pain came back, something beeped loudly and it went fuzzy again.

The next time it felt clearer. Same place, hospital bed, and I was on my own, but as soon as I tried to move I was surrounded by nurses and soon after that Jack came back. When the nurses had finished poking me about, wiping me down and giving me pills, Jack sat on my bed.

'This isn't the happy ending,' he said.

'Why?' Although I never thought anything would be happy again.

'I can't find Mary,' Jack blurted.

Mary had been with us through so much of this mess. Jack and Mary together. It hadn't always been easy. Jenna probably didn't miss her, but Jack obviously had such strong feelings for Mary. He'd told me on the coach that he wouldn't see her again. But that was because he believed we were all going to die. Maybe he thought he had a chance finding that we were still alive.

I waited. He didn't say anything; his face gave away nothing but a blank stare.

'Is there more? Was it Demelza? What did she do?' I asked after several minutes of silence. Whatever they were giving me through this drip was still making my mind blank out from time to time.

'No, she's disappeared.'

It took me a moment to realise Jack was still talking about Mary.

'But how did we get out of the war? How did we get back here?' I asked.

'Yes, it was Demelza,' Jack said. 'Jenna told me that after a few days' farming Demelza was even more impossible than usual. I think Jen was trying to work out a way to get her shot.'

At that moment, Jenna appeared. She was in uniform, all sorts of army ribbons and stars, she came with three other soldiers who stood to attention at the end of my bed.

'Leave,' Jenna barked at them.

The soldiers shuffled nervously.

'I said, leave,' Jenna was right in the face of one of them.

'But, ma'am, General Zach said we were never to leave you alone,' the soldier, aged at least thirteen, replied.

Jenna's shoulders dropped. She turned to me, 'Good to have you back, soldier.' She patted my arm, 'Soon have you back to normal.' She raised her eyebrows and then looked at Jack. 'I'll let the sergeant explain.' With that she stood and marched out of the ward with her soldiers scrabbling to follow.

'What?' I said. Watching Jenna leave.

Jack did the explaining.

Jenna and Demelza had been moved soon after I had left the prison cell on the edge of the moor. They joined other girls and ended up on a farm, growing potatoes and doing other things that were meant to be secret. Jenna had said she quite liked the farm, but Demelza whined all the time. That ended up with Jenna pushing her into a ditch.

'I think we've done that to Demelza before,' I said, something coming into my head through my drug-induced haze.

Something else wasn't right. I'd only seen young women – girls – working in the fields. But they weren't sending women to fight at the front. So, they couldn't all have been killed. Where were they? And it wasn't all of them, what about the nurses in here. I had a load of questions and Jack was still explaining.

'That's when Demelza told Jenna about the rats.' Jack talking about rats pulled me back to listening.

'Rats, the Black Death. Loads of rats then,' I said, blurring my words. I tried to sit up but was too weak. 'But Jack, do you remember? When I met you on the bus, you didn't seem to remember anything, nothing about the time travel and Miss Tregarthur.'

'It came back to me when I talked with Matt and Stevie. We pieced together what had happened after Miss Tregarthur's hike on the moor,' Jack said.

'And the rats?' I asked.

'Yeah, apparently Zach developed a rat phobia,' Jack lowered his voice.

'Strange, I thought he was one.' My attempt to laugh echoed in the ward.

'You have to speak quietly.' Jack moved up the bed. 'If this gets out, then we have no chance.'

'But lots of people have phobias about rats.' I couldn't see why this could be important.

'Ah, but not like our dear Supreme Commander's phobia,' Jack sneered. 'You give him a rat and he falls apart, screaming, wailing, climbing under the furniture, completely uncontrollable.'

I liked that idea, it was definitely what Zach deserved. I imagined what I would do if I recovered enough to find him, to find Zach and a sack of rats. That thought must have taken my mind off for a few seconds.

Jack had continued to talk, '… he kept it quiet, used his army to make sure there were never rats about, but he said it was for hygiene reasons, couldn't let the army boss get sick.'

'That explains the poison,' I added.

'Yep,' Jack said. 'That was Zach's men spraying everything with rat poison when he was expected to give out medals.'

'But, so, what?' I said. 'Why is that important? Why does it matter if Zach doesn't particularly like rats? How could that help?'

'Zach turned up at the farm,' Jack explained. 'He'd come to gloat over Demelza and Jenna. He'd have enjoyed that except he took his new girlfriend. Actually, it might have been her idea, maybe she wanted to make sure that Zach really didn't still want to be with Demelza.'

A nurse arrived with another pill and a glass of water. She told Jack he couldn't sit on the bed. Jack stood until she left.

'Anyway, after Zach had done his gloating, Officer Harper, as she was then, stayed behind and ramped up the insults. Jen reckons she was trying to get Demelza to attack her so that she could have her shot. They're all pretty gun-happy.'

'And?'

Demelza whispered about the rats and that made Harper -

Zach's girlfriend or Officer Harper who had become Viscount Harper – that made some light switch on in her brain. The next day Harper came back to the farm, on the quiet and took Demelza and Jenna away.

'Jenna knew about the rats?'

'I guess Jenna used a bit more violence to find out,' Jack laughed and I remembered other times when Jenna had made Demelza give her information.

Jack looked around the room. There were no other patients in this small ward and the nurses had gone. Jack still got up and went to the door to check if we were alone and to make sure that no one was listening. There was a glazed glass window on the end wall, which must have led to the nurses, we could hear them talking and a few noises of banging – that had something to do with bedpans – there must have been other patients somewhere in this hospital. Jack came back.

'After Demelza had gone over the problem about Zach, this Harper decided to set him up. She and the two girls went up to his barracks ...'

'Why did she take Jenna and Demelza, why did she need them?'

'Not too clear on that. I think she didn't completely believe them,' Jack said. 'She was going to let them show her. I suppose if it hadn't worked she'd have made something up about them escaping and we'd be back to having them shot.'

'But it worked?'

'Oh yes, it worked. Jenna was the one with a sack of rats. They burst into his room and Jenna set them lose before Zach could do anything. Blind panic is the way she described what happened. Zach started screaming, trying to get out, but they'd locked the door. He tried to get under a bed, still screaming and thrashing about. Lucky that he had his own private block or the whole army would have turned up hearing the noise Zach made.'

'I love it, but so what, so what if they scared the pants off him, what does that matter? No one else would know, not exactly as if this Harper had got it ...'

I looked up at Jack and saw his smile, 'Got it on her phone? Taken a video?' Jack took another look around the empty room. 'But she had. That's exactly what she did, took out her phone and videoed the whole thing. They had to wait for ages until the rats found a way to get out of the room. Jenna and Demelza were in stitches. Harper had left, but soon came back and said she'd posted the video on the net.'

I stared at Jack with my mouth open. That was going to take some explaining. We seemed to be in the time of the First World War and here was someone with a mobile phone.

'Harper threatened to show everyone the video unless he made her a Viscount,' Jack explained. 'Not sure what a Viscount is, but it seems to work. She's the one telling everyone what to do.'

'Why didn't Zach have her killed?' I didn't think Zach would care if his new girlfriend died after the rat incident.

'Harper said she'd given it to the Americans, they agreed some sort of deal with Zach. He's still meant to be in charge, it's just that the orders are going to come from Harper. She still keeps a few rats, just in case.'

Videos and the internet? It all sounded good to me but Jack's smile had disappeared – thoughts of Mary must have returned.

-7-

VISCOUNT HARPER

Over the days it took me to recover, I spent most of my time alone. Jenna came again with her soldier-followers, Jack came and this time with followers of his own. But they couldn't stay for long or say very much. Jenna was able to tell me that we'd been brought back as heroes.

'It was all I could do,' Jenna nodded her head at her soldiers, clear that she was not free to explain. 'We brought you back as heroes. It happens with medal winners, they travel round the country and persuade people that the war is going well.'

'Does that work?' I asked.

'No.'

'What happens after that?' I looked at Jenna and could see in her eyes, we were going to be sent back to the war. 'But ...' I stopped.

'What?' I could see Jenna worried what I might be about to ask.

'It's just ... why aren't there any old women? And the nurses?' Jenna looked relieved, this was something she could talk about. 'The nurses are all from abroad, lots of them have trained in America, it's part of their effort to support us.'

'But what happened to all the other women, if they don't send them to fight, where have they all gone?'

Jenna might be ok talking about nurses, but this was a more difficult area: 'There are some older women, but ...' Jenna lowered her voice, 'this whole thing isn't like normal real, it has to be ...' she whispered, 'Miss Tregarthur.'

I needed to talk to Jenna alone, but that wasn't going to happen. She might be a Field Marshal but she seemed more of a prisoner. Even if we had escaped from the war for a while, nothing was going to be easy. It had always been a problem – dealing with Zach's girlfriends.

The next day Viscount Harper arrived and she was on her own. I was just out of bed, trying to see if I could walk on my injured leg. I was being helped by the nurses, but Harper ordered them to leave and me back to my bed.

'Getting better,' Harper said and it sounded more like an order than a question.

'Can I see the video?' I thought it was worth a try.

'You know about phones?'

I didn't answer but I suppose my face gave me away.

'How?' she demanded, but I still didn't answer. I'm not sure why. If she had a mobile phone, then she was obviously from a future rather than whatever time we were meant to be here. But it didn't feel right, didn't feel safe, to tell this person the whole story. She definitely hadn't cared about us when we first met. I thought she was probably only interested in herself, whatever she could gain, and I wasn't going to give her anything.

'Tomorrow, we'll talk.' She strode out of the ward.

When tomorrow came, they wheeled me out of the ward in a

real wheelchair. I think I could have walked but they weren't going to let me. I was taken down corridors past other wards and these were not empty. Clearly the war brought back enough casualties to keep this place going. The beds were full of patients with their arms and legs strung up in slings. But somehow, they didn't look quite right, the bandages had slipped. I'd only seen nurses, where were the doctors? What age were they? If they couldn't fix machines, how did they train doctors and nurses? Why was I the only person in my ward – I supposed that was to do with Zach and the rats. For some reason the made-up Viscount Harper seemed to have done all this. Why?

As I was wheeled past the other wards I could see we were at least one floor up in this building. It wasn't as though this was a modern hospital. The walls were painted a hideous green, the floor some grey shining stuff, old radiators, old lights. The hospital felt old and not in a great condition. That fitted with what Jack had said about things not being repaired, broken machines. This was still a place from the same time as the war.

I was taken down in an old lift. It was difficult to get an idea when this lift might have been made. I tried to ask one of the soldiers who had been sent to get me.

'It's just a lift, lucky it works,' he said.

'How old is it?' I tried again.

'Old,' he replied. 'Everything is old.'

I didn't get any more information. We wheeled out of a door, along a path and into another brick building. Wherever we were this was all army property. There were signs about the war everywhere and instructions not to spread rumours, soldiers posted at each corner. Our destination was a large room, concrete floor, no carpet, no curtains, bright lights, and a large table. It looked like the sort of room you would use for interrogation – and not with polite questions. Jenna, Demelza, Jack and Matt sat around a table on iron chairs, bolted to the floor. I was wheeled up to join them.

I wondered where Stevie might be but Viscount Harper barged through the doors before I had a chance to ask.

'Out,' she ordered the guard who came with her. Harper strode to the table, took out a gun from a holster on her hip, sat on the only other chair, slapping the gun against her palm making it obvious that she might use it at any time. Use it to shoot us.

'I need some answers,' she demanded.

Actually, I thought it was us who needed answers. There was far too much going on here, but I didn't think we were going to find out anything.

'You, Alvin, tell me who you really are.' Harper pointed her gun at me.

'We don't talk until you let us go,' Jenna answered for me.

'Not going to happen.' Harper turned the gun towards Jenna. 'It's probable that you're all spies and that's a death sentence.'

'We've survived death sentences before,' I decided I was going to talk. Jenna shot me a look.

'When?' Harper snapped, and when she did there was a twang to her voice. It made me think.

'When was that Jen? The last death sentence. Must have been … a few hundred years ago, difficult to say unless you know what year it is now,' I said.

'1917,' Harper said.

'1917 and mobile phones? I don't think so,' I laughed.

'That must mean you are spies,' Harper looked unsettled.

This wasn't going the way she wanted it to go.

'You're American.' Jack looked up, surprised that he knew this, he'd also spotted the twang.

'Never,' she said, obviously shaken by Jack's guess. 'Just picked up the accent from talking to the American delegation we had here.'

'Don't believe you,' Demelza decided to join in. 'Anyway, now you've got that video of Zach, you've taken over, what's going to happen next? Have you got any plan at all, except liking being in charge?'

It didn't look as though Harper had much of a plan, certainly nothing to stop the war.

'But I am sending you to America.' Harper rose from her seat. 'I'm calling for a plane, tomorrow, then the real questions will start. It is a one-way flight. I'll say you're Russians, they'll like that. That's why you're all still alive.' Harper went for the door and called the soldiers back.

'We're keeping you in this block, until you go. Individual cells. It's more secure. No way out.' Harper left.

We didn't move. It seemed that the soldiers weren't ready to take us to our cells.

'Anyone any idea about anything?' I looked round our group.

'Too much to explain,' Jenna answered. 'We need to get out of here, if they ship us off to America then there's no chance of stopping Miss Tregarthur.'

The guard of soldiers were looking nervous at this stage. All of them were armed. I didn't want them to learn of our plans, but this might be the only chance we had to talk.

'Aren't you a Field Marshal?' I asked. 'Surely you can order them to let us go?' I waved my hand at the soldiers.

'Harper just made up the titles so we could stay where she wanted us. We didn't have to go back to the farm, she made out we had important plans for the war. She still made sure we couldn't go anywhere without an escort.'

'I couldn't go anywhere at all,' Demelza whined and pointed at Jenna. 'She made sure of that.'

Jenna shrugged. 'We've got to tell her, tell Harper the whole story and see if she believes us. It's the only chance we've got.'

Silence followed before I nodded. We didn't look at the others.

Jenna called to the guard, 'Get Viscount Harper back.'

The soldiers didn't look as though they were going to do anything.

'Tell her we need to talk,' Jenna said loudly. 'If you don't get her, then it's back to the front for all of you.'

I wasn't sure if they believed her, but she had been a supposed Field Marshal and that appeared to be enough. A while later Harper returned, back with the gun and sending the other soldiers away.

So, Jenna told her the story of Miss Tregarthur and our travels in time. We'd done this before, told someone the story. They hadn't believed it.

'Rubbish,' Harper laughed. 'I knew you were spies.' But, again, her voice betrayed her. There must have been enough in our story to make her wonder.

'You know that phone you've got?' Jenna nodded towards her and Harper instinctively patted her top pocket. 'Yes, that one,' Jenna went on. 'The one you're going to use to call America.'

'How did…' Harper stopped herself.

'I guess it uses satellites, American satellites,' Jack joined in. I was glad we had an expert. Harper was silent, obviously confused, and looked a bit scared.

'Can you Google things on it?' Jenna pointed at the pocket.

'What … Google?' Harper stammered.

'Just try,' Jenna demanded.

Harper took out the phone and looked at it, not seeming to know what to do.

'Let me,' Jack held out his hand.

I could see this was the moment it was either going to go seriously wrong or Harper might actually help. Harper was staring at Jack's hand, slowly she passed over the phone.

Jack poked around for a while on the phone. 'No Google, but there is another search engine, Dogpile.' Jack stood and went over to Harper. 'Look, I've typed in Miss Tregarthur.' He handed the phone back.

Up on the screen came the news about Miss Tregarthur and her school hike, how she had led a group of teenagers onto the moor and they had disappeared. This was more than weird. I had no idea how a modern phone could search for the time we'd set out on that first walk, when it was meant to be 1917 here and in the middle of a war. I guess that wasn't as weird as the idea of time travel.

Harper spent ages staring at her phone. Then she spoke rather slowly. 'What if I do believe you? Why should I help you?'

'Aren't you trying to stop this war?' Jenna folded her arms.

'Of course, it's just …' Harper slowed to a stop.

'It's just you can't,' Jenna went on. 'This is all about the rules, isn't it?'

Harper nodded with her lips held tightly in a glum look.

'You Americans can't join in on our side or the Russians will join in on the German side. The rest of the world has agreed to stand back and watch.' It was Jack who spoke, he had a better grasp of the problem.

'Everyone knows that,' Harper said. 'The war bubble they call it, just hangs over this part of Europe, a time loop.'

'What about the women?' Jenna butted in.

'What women?' Harper looked surprised.

'There aren't any old women,' I said. 'Where are they?'

'We're trying to find out, it could be …' Harper stopped and didn't sound as though she wanted to explain.

'You think it's related to the cavemen.' Jack had obviously been thinking about this. I couldn't see what he meant.

'How can you know about that?' Harper snapped.

'She's swapping them,' Jenna had grasped what Jack meant. 'She's broken time, brought these cavemen from thousands of years in the past, and she's swapped them with people in this time. It just happens that there were more women to swap, that's what she's done. That's how she's done it, one in, one out.'

'How could anyone do that?' Harper said.

'You've guessed that's what's happening?' Jack said.

'But they don't know about Miss Tregarthur and how she's messed up time to make this work.' Jenna sat forward in her chair. 'If we can stop her then it all ends.'

I could see that something was changing in Harper's mind. It was difficult to know what that might be, or if it was likely to be entirely bad.

'And how do you do that? How can you lot stop a war?' Harper sneered.

'You let us go,' I smiled, hoping we were winning.

'Never.' Harper stood. 'It's lock up time.'

'And the cavemen?' I watched for any reaction, and I was sure she tried to hide something. 'Aren't they covered by the rules? You seem to be using American planes and helicopters over the moor.'

'And chasing us,' Jenna added.

Harper sat down again, looking serious. 'What do you know about the cavemen?'

'They're part of Miss Tregarthur's mess, can't you see that?' Jenna would have poked Harper if she'd been closer.

'I can't talk about them,' Harper said. 'It's top secret, a matter for American intelligence. It doesn't matter if you don't tell me all about it – they'll soon get the truth from you when you get state-side. They don't care about using torture.'

'So, you are an American spy?' Demelza joined in for the first time. 'Do many people know that?'

Demelza was a real expert in finding people's weak points. And Harper wasn't great at hiding them. She slapped her hand over her mouth, obviously realising she had said too much.

'It's just that I was thinking of sending a text.' No one had noticed that Demelza had managed to hold on to Harper's phone. 'Harper: American Spy unmasked,' Demelza read from the screen. 'I was thinking of using "send all". I think I just need to press "enter", if that's alright.' Her finger hovered over the button.

Harper jerked forward trying to snatch the phone, but Demelza just leant back and gave a Demelza sneered laugh. 'Oh, by the way I was sending that with the recording of our last conversation about torture.' Demelza paused, holding up the phone. 'Just amazing, this is really quite new. I think we should hold on to it.'

'The Americans must have a network installed here,' Jack said. 'Another secret, maybe.'

Harper was looking hot and flushed.

'You let us go,' I said again and I could see she was trying to think her way out of this.

'You let us go and we'll give it back to you,' Demelza waved the phone in the air.

'I'll just call the guards, soon take it back,' Harper's voice was not confident.

'Make one move and I send the text,' Demelza said, and her words echoed round the room.

Harper's face fell, I could see the tears in her eyes. With the rat story, she had set herself up as a Viscount, whatever that was. It felt as though she had pretty much taken over from Zach.

Maybe that was what the Americans wanted, some other part of their plan. Did we have a chance to ruin all this? Harper was defeated. We set about working out what we should do. Demelza kept her hands on the phone.

SCOUTING PARTY

Eventually, with our permission, we were all moved to the canteen. Well, it was Demelza's permission, she was loving this. I did wonder if Demelza was thinking about staying here. She'd have more plans for Zach. More revenge plans.

The idea was simple. Wait for darkness. Harper would set off some emergency siren at the other end of the building. The soldiers guarding us would all run off to see what was happening. All we had to do was to get through the kitchen and find the car she would leave outside.

'And you leave the phone on the table,' Harper had said, hopefully.

'No way,' Jenna replied. 'We don't get rid of the phone until we are well out of here.'

Harper hadn't an answer for that, just a worried face.

'You can come with us,' Jenna suggested.

Harper looked up, 'Where to?'

'Just until we get away, then we give you the phone and you live happily ever after,' Jenna gave the sweetest of smiles. I was glad she did that, there was no way we could let Harper loose after she'd got the phone.

Harper still nodded, 'I'll be in the car.'

'What happens if your guard soldiers don't follow the

siren?' Jack said.

'These soldiers are about twelve years old, just shout "boo" at them and they'll run,' Harper had nodded towards the soldiers. They were so smart in their army uniforms, smart and so very young. Young, nervous and armed. I didn't like it.

'Slip us your gun,' I pointed at the weapon that was still lying on the table in front of Harper.

Harper pursed her lips. 'Not loaded anyway.'

The gun seemed to end up in Jenna's hands.

Stevie joined us.

'They wanted some German translation,' he said. 'I'm useful, sometimes.' I could see tears in his eyes. Stevie didn't often feel useful – just used. I did worry about Stevie – the war had scrambled his brain, he was muttering a lot to himself, muttering in German. If we ever got him home I hoped he would recover from all that had happened. I just wasn't sure what 'recovered' might mean. Maybe he'd go back to whining. Would we all go back to how we had been? I had changed a lot, I wasn't sure if it was for the better, even if Jenna had told me it was.

Matt had stayed silent throughout the talk with Harper. Matt was usually silent so that wasn't new. I had to hope the two of them would be strong enough to see us through this plan.

We had a whole lot of time to think and worry as we sat around a table, waiting for dark and the siren. From time to time other soldiers came in to eat in the canteen, but mostly the place was empty – apart from four guards who were left to watch us.

Harper explained that she couldn't leave us alone. 'Too suspicious,' she said.

I wasn't too worried about the guards. They all looked as though they were about to wet themselves. Jenna had given me the gun. Harper was wrong – it was loaded. There was more going on than I knew. I didn't plan to shoot any of these kids, but I could threaten them.

The siren was at the other end of the block, but it still started with a deafening wail. A group of soldiers had come into the canteen. In seconds the place emptied, chairs flung back on the ground as all of them ran.

Our four guards looked at each other, but still ran for it. Although the siren had not been used for some time, we later found out it signalled an air-raid. Apparently, when the German air-ships had been working they had to plan for bombing attacks. These soldiers were making for the shelter, apparently the shelter was near the siren. Staying alive was more important than guarding us.

We were alone. Even the kitchen staff had left. We walked out past steel benches, huge vats of stew, loads of washing up, and through a door into the car park, hazy with dim street lights which started to go out – must have been part of the air raid precautions to leave the place in darkness.

One of the cars flashed its headlights. Harper had kept to her word. We made for the vehicle.

Harper sat in the driving seat of a huge American Humvee. She drove off as soon as we'd scrambled inside. She didn't talk until we were through the gate, no stopping. Every one of the soldiers had disappeared to find the shelter.

'I put Zach's name on the instructions for the emergency drill,' Harper gave a slight giggle. I think she was enjoying this.

Even being a Viscount was probably not enough. 'Where are we going?' she asked.

'Dartmoor,' Jenna said. 'Back to the place we met, before you sent Alvin off to the war.'

'Oh, by the way,' Harper said in a matter of fact voice. 'There's someone else hidden in the back.'

I reached for the gun but I didn't need it.

'Mary,' Jack yelled and dived between the seats to get to her. Ages passed before they came up for air.

'Well if a Viscount can't find someone, then I don't see the point,' Harper said with a smile while she swerved to avoid a pot hole. Jack and Mary were wittering on like an old couple. We left them to it.

It wasn't a quick drive; several hours of dodging holes in a road that hadn't seen repairs for some time. I was in the front with Harper, the others in the back were playing with anything they could find, like the heating and windows, until they found that a screen on the back of my seat actually worked and Demelza managed to find a DVD which played cartoons. Mickey Mouse screamed out our return to a more modern life in the car, while 1917 was playing outside.

Hours later it was getting light as we reached the fence around the moor. Harper drove on smaller roads, less used and actually in better condition than the main routes. The Humvee had a satnav, Harper found the road leading to the army buildings we'd been taken to when we came down from the moor.

'What now?' Harper stopped and turned to us. I had no idea. The problem was that no one else had either. We'd been too set on escaping without thinking this through.

'We have to get back up to the Hanging Stones,' Jenna said after a while.

'You want to get out on the moor?' Harper said as though it was the most stupid idea she'd heard. 'Those cavemen kill anything that moves out there. That's why ...' She stopped.

'Why you Americans are trying to kill them?' Jenna said.

Harper nodded, 'More studying them, but they're all vicious, won't do anything else, just attack. And ... I'm definitely not supposed to talk about this, but if you do kill them, more just reappear, almost as if they come out of the ground.'

'Are they new cavemen or just the same ones?' Jack leant forward in his seat. I wasn't sure what he was getting at.

'You know that?' Harper stammered.

'It's Miss Tregarthur and the mess of time,' Jack went on. 'It's a never-ending loop. Like the war goes on, but different. I guess if you kill the cavemen, they disappear at the end of one time cycle and then reappear.'

Harper gave a sharp intake of breath.

'That's probably why the Americans are so interested in them, trying to find out why it happens. That right?' Jack asked Harper, who nodded silently.

'But ...' Mary stopped.

'What?' Jenna.

Mary went on: 'If Miss Tregarthur is swapping people and cavemen, well how do we get everyone back in their own time – like your mum said we had to do?'

That was much too weird for me to understand.

'I guess we just have to get back to the time before she started this,' Jenna shrugged. 'Right now, we have to get to the Hanging Stones. How can we get over the fence?'

'If you try that, it sets off an alarm.' Harper turned to Jenna. 'One of ours.'

'You're admitting to being American?' Jen laughed. 'Is there any other way?'

'Not here,' Harper replied. 'This fence goes all the way around the moor. There's no one living inside and the place is overrun with cavemen. That's why it's alarmed. If they try to break through then we send out the jets or the helicopters. We have a base on the other side, but it's only for flying. We don't have a gate – just too dangerous.'

'We got out,' I said. 'Just ran off the moor and through the gate.'

'That's the only gate on this side,' Harper said. 'That's where the soldiers stay, keeping watch, if there's anything suspicious happening they usually just shoot – you were lucky you met a scouting group.'

I didn't feel lucky and wondered what sort of scouts they had.

'They're called scouts because they go out looking around for things – it's called scouting,' Jack explained to me. And there was me thinking it was about getting badges. Mind you these soldiers looked more like boy-scouts.

'Harper,' Jenna put her hand on the Viscount's shoulder. 'I've no idea what being a Viscount means, but it seems pretty important. And I'm wearing the uniform of a field Marshal and Demelza here is obviously an Admiral,' Jenna laughed as Demelza tried to puff herself up in an important way. 'We go into this army place, tell them we have to do a mission and get them to escort us on to the moor.'

Harper shrugged, 'Give it a try.' And she drove off.

I wasn't sure why she hadn't asked for her phone. I suppose

she'd worked out that we couldn't give it back to her. We had no other hold over her. That meant we were stuck with her. I just hoped that if we got back to the Hanging Stones then we could escape from this place. There was an obvious flaw in that idea – Miss Tregarthur was the tunnel, why would she do anything to help us?

Harper drew into the army compound and hooted. The giant American Humvee made its presence known. Soldiers came running out of every hut, shouting orders that had them forming lines and saluting. These soldiers wanted to make sure we saw they were well disciplined. They knew this was an easy job, guarding this moor gate, rather than getting shot in a trench.

We got out, with Harper, Jenna and Demelza all saluting back. Harper looked a bit bewildered. So did Matt and Stevie. Jack was still holding on to Mary – neither of them seemed to care what happened.

Jenna marched up to the most senior looking soldier – he was a different Major to the one we'd met before, 'You. Take us to your meeting room and bring your lead scout soldier.'

We were led into one of the huts. I could see Jenna looking for the vending machine but we didn't see one this time.

Jenna seemed to feel she should take charge, demanding an armed group to take us out to the Hanging Stones.

'B… b … but that's where they come out from,' one of the scouts stuttered. 'The cavemen pile out from the rocks, hundreds of them, they'll kill us all.'

Jack turned to Harper, 'I guess that happens at the same time, maybe every day, maybe a week or a month later – that's the loop.'

'Not always,' said the scout. 'Sometimes it just happens.'

The Major spoke, 'We have made up a sort of timetable. It's usually a week, a Monday, when they seem to pour out of the ground.'

'But Major,' interrupted the scout. 'It's been different, yesterday we saw it happen and that was Wednesday. We think it's becoming more random.'

I wondered about that. Was this changing because of us? Was there some way that Miss Tregarthur knew we were on our way? How could that be? She might be the time tunnel, taken up by the rocks of the moor, but she'd died. This tunnel had to have brought her back to some sort of life. The idea of a zombie Miss Tregarthur was too terrible to even think about.

While I had been dreaming about Miss Tregarthur, Jenna had overridden the scout and arranged for us to go out, 'NOW.' She'd banged the table. And we did. We set out as an army patrol. They gave each of us a pack with emergency supplies and rations.

The heavily defended gate squeaked open as our group went into the wood. A strange group. Almost like another school hike, except we were dressed in army uniforms. Jack still wouldn't let go of Mary's hand. We had ten armed soldiers with us. Well, ten armed young people looking terrified, jumping at every noise. I suppose taking them with us might have provided us some protection, at least the cavemen could chase them rather than us, but I would have preferred American helicopters. Harper had been vague on why that was impossible. I felt as though she had a plan that she had not discussed yet. A plan that didn't involve more of her countrymen.

We came to the old wire fence that we'd jumped over before. All was quiet. The scout soldiers were scanning the hills for any sign of cavemen. Over the fence, we started up the hill – Hanging Stone Hill – we knew it well. All was quiet, but the going was so slow, scouts continually stopping and saying, 'What's that?' at nothing. The ground became wetter as we neared the flat summit, we were into the black peaty mud of Dartmoor, squelching with each step.

We did hear some real sounds, howls way out in the distance. Reminded me of dogs; we'd met wild dogs out here. Wild dogs and dead bodies in the time of the Black Death. Harper said there were only cavemen out here. I wondered what they lived off. Were mammoths in this loop with them or even those tigers that had killed off many of Crow's tribe? He'd once been the caveman on our side, until one of the others had clubbed him to death. I thought of all the other dangers we'd faced, time travelling through thousands of years on this moor. What would we find now?

Over the crest of the hill, we could look out over the bleak landscape. A mist was forming in the valley below and starting to waft up towards us. There was dampness in the air, but no storm yet. Looking out I couldn't see any movement, not even sheep grazing. The moor was empty. Ahead were the strange stones, one looking as though it was balanced on another. But that was just an illusion. It was only one stone, or so it had seemed until Miss Tregarthur was dragged into the ground, then the stones had come apart, forming a giant pincer. That flashback made me shiver. But surely they were just stones; stones and silence.

The rest of us held back.

Jenna walked forward and shouted, 'Bring the tunnel, you must take us home.' Her words simply echoed into the distance. The scout soldiers started muttering, obviously thinking we were stupid. Stupid to be shouting to these stones, shouting about going home.

'No crystal, no tunnel,' Demelza said unhelpfully.

'Give me the gun,' Jenna held out her hand to me and I passed over Harper's weapon. I had kept it with me all the time but hadn't needed to shoot anyone in our escape. Lucky because I wasn't sure I could have shot any of these young soldiers.

Jenna turned back to the stones and fired into the ground, 'Get me the tunnel,' she shouted. Nothing happened. The mist of the moor had risen up all around us. We could barely see more than a few yards, but this was ordinary mist, not something to show the opening of the time tunnel.

Jenna fired again and smashed the gun down on to the stones and shouted.

I felt something. The ground seemed to tremble under my feet. A sound filled my head. I knew it at once.

Miss Tregarthur's screech, it came up from the Hanging Stones: 'You will never leave. You will die, you will die.'

The tremble grew stronger, a mist of red oozed out from around the rocks. A roaring sound swept across the moor, coming towards us as it had done before. The sound became a scream, below us the ground opened in a wide fissure. This was not an earthquake or the time tunnel opening. This was Miss Tregarthur's loop. With louder screams and howls, club wielding cavemen leapt up, pouring out of the gap in the moor.

'Run,' screamed the lead scout and our soldiers sprinted off. They might be young soldiers but that didn't stop them being fast runners. We were slower, not sure of what to do.

'Not that way,' Jenna shouted, when I did start to follow the soldiers. Jenna waved us in the opposite way, right into the thickest of the moor's mist. Stevie didn't move until Matt grabbed him.

Jenna was searching for something. 'Can't find it, we'll have to go down.'

We stumbled down the side of the hill, slipping and sliding, tripping over clumps of grass, leaping to avoid deep pools of black water.

Perhaps we were hidden by the mist, but the cavemen seemed to have chased after the soldiers. We were not going to stop and find out if there were more behind us. We ran on. All of us, including Harper. On and on, but slowing as we found deeper, wetter, boggy ground; all the time the mist was getting thicker. We stopped. The mist was too thick to find our way. If it lifted then I didn't think we were far enough away from the cavemen. If we stayed here they would see us.

'We must go on.' I peered ahead, hoping to see something, but only occasional rocks stood out from the moor, rocks that looked like people. Hard not to imagine each one was a caveman waiting to attack.

'We can't see anything,' Jenna sounded hopeless. 'We'll just end up going in circles.'

'Follow the light,' Jack shouted and pointed. 'That way is lighter than behind us, if we keep going that way we are following the sun, that should at least keep us on a straight line.'

I could just about see what Jack meant. Ahead was a little lighter, but only just. We tried to follow it, but had to keep stopping, uncertain whether we were still heading in the right direction. The ground started to drop in front of us, down we went, tumbling as the slope grew steeper.

Ahead I heard a splash and a shout. Jack was leading and had fallen into water at the bottom of the hill. We were in a valley I remembered from another time. Once before there had been a hut, with a dead body. There was no hut anymore. I hoped we weren't going to provide the dead bodies.

Walking on, the mist started to lift, clearing as we came down from the high moor. Suddenly the valley opened out, we were in the open, above us an almost cloudless blue sky. The weather changes on this moor were incredible. I looked behind, there was almost nothing to see. The thick blanket of misty cloud still hung over the tors. But with a stronger wind the cloud everywhere was starting to lift. Soon anyone higher up would be able to see us.

'Faster,' I shouted. We had to get away before the cavemen spotted us. That was if the only members of this wild tribe were behind us. For all I knew there might be more of them ahead.

'Make for the cave,' Jenna called and I knew where she meant us to go. She meant us to head for the stream we had followed before. The stream and the cave that led to a house. The house of Baylock Tregarthur. The Tregarthur home. Not a good place to go, not a place of safety.

9

BAYLOCK'S RUIN

Before long the valley grew narrower. We followed the stream, picking our way, searching the bank on the other side, and from time to time looking back to see if we were being followed. The bank became steeper, rocky, becoming a cliff as we went further down.

'There,' Jenna stopped and pointed to some dripping rocks on the other side of the stream.

'What?' Mary, Matt, Stevie and Jack called together. They were looking at a dark, wet opening, half covered with fallen branches and bushes.

'That's the way to the Tregarthur cave.' Jenna was looking for somewhere to cross.

'What? In there?' said Jack, looking at Mary, who shrugged.

Matt and Stevie didn't seem too surprised. They didn't ask as many questions as Jack and Mary, especially when they knew it concerned Miss Tregarthur, as though they knew it would be too weird. So, tunnels and caves were probably almost normal to them, even if they had no idea where they were going.

But Harper asked: 'Why are we going in there?'

'We need a crystal,' I replied.

We hadn't explained to the others where we were headed or why.

'There's a route into the hillside. A path beside another small stream leads underground. If we follow it, then it comes to a cave we found before ...' I started.

'A path? Really?' Harper looked over the stream.

'Well, it's a tunnel,' I hadn't wanted to say 'tunnel'. We'd had too much trouble with tunnels.

Demelza had spent more time here than us. 'There's more than a cave,' she said. 'There's a whole lot of tunnels in there. They don't just lead to a cave, they go up to the house ...' She stopped. Demelza must have realised she would give too much away. There were things we still didn't know about her time with Miss Tregarthur.

Jenna took over, 'Up there, somewhere.' She pointed up the hill. 'There's an old house that belonged to the Tregarthurs. We ended up there in another time. There was an old man.'

'Baylock,' I added.

'Yeah,' Jenna went on. 'Baylock Tregarthur; one of her relatives.'

'The other members of the family tried to tell us they were different, not like Miss Tregarthur.' I chucked a stone into the river; it bounced on a rock and shot into the opening, echoing in the dark. 'I'm not sure they were better. Baylock seemed to be in charge. But it all went wrong,' Jenna broke in. 'Last time we were in the house it came under attack from the cavemen. I think that was the start of the real mess in time – cavemen, the war, the time loop. We fell right into it after we escaped from the house.'

'OK,' Harper paused. 'You want us to go into this place that is probably full of wild angry savages, or if not, then wild angry Tregarthurs in your crazy time lady's home?'

'About right,' Jenna tried to make it sound lighter than it was.

'No choice,' I said and we heard more howls from out on the moor.

I still wasn't sure why Harper was still with us. We had no reason to trust her and no reason for having her along.

'You don't have to come,' I said to her. 'You could just go back and run the army with Zach?'

'Oh, I'm having too much fun.' Harper didn't smile. I guessed that escaping with us probably meant she couldn't go back; maybe the Americans wouldn't want her either.

'Can we stop here for a while?' Mary suggested. 'I mean we can listen and see if we hear anything from inside that,' she pointed. The opening looked even less promising as it was starting to get dark.

That seemed a good idea, but would we be any safer out here?

'There's another overhang in the cliff.' Jack had crossed over the stream.

I didn't think we had much choice. We were all too exhausted, and without any further argument we crossed over to Jack and huddled under the overhang. At least it wasn't raining.

It was time to find out what the army had put in our packs. We were lucky. The American involvement on the moor didn't just extend to the vending machine. We had some self-heating stew and more chocolate bars, but I can't say it was a great evening picnic. From time to time, wild howls came down to us from the high moor. The cavemen were up there and they didn't sound happy. At least they sounded a long way off.

'How does this crystal thing work?' Harper asked after we'd eaten most of what we had, despite Mary trying to get us to save some of the food.

It was good having sensible Mary back with us. Mary and Jack had solved most of the problems we'd ever had. It had been a long time since I had thought about anything other than surviving, but sitting by this stream, my mind drifted off. Was Mum really dead? I knew Dad and my older brother were in jail, what would happen if I did get home? Out on the street had been the only option.

I jerked back into reality, hearing another caveman howl and Jenna explaining more: '... these crystals are part of the time tunnel. I thought there was only one but there may be more, I'm hoping we might find something in the house, if there's anything left of it.'

'I still don't see how you control the tunnel with a crystal,' Harper said again.

'No idea how it works,' Jenna started.

'It's when you hit it,' I added because Jenna seemed not to want to explain that.

'Yes, the crystals seem to be part of the time tunnel, almost as if they were alive.' Jenna stopped again.

'When Miss Tregarthur smashed something down on the crystal, it set off a terrible scream that came from the Hanging Stones,' I said. 'It's a noise you never want to hear again. The tunnel screams in pain when you damage the crystal. You'll know that when you hear the scream.'

'So, the time tunnel does what you want to stop the pain - nice.' Mary looked away.

'If we find a crystal, then I hope we can just use the threat of damaging it,' Jenna tried to make it sound better than it was. I didn't care if we hurt Miss Tregarthur, even if Mary might care. I looked at Jenna and saw the shake of her head.

Neither of us wanted to explain that we thought the tunnel was at least partly human, or was the spirit of Miss Tregarthur. If the crystal worked then it would be her that was screaming. I thought Jenna was being oversensitive, a lot had happened to Mary, she was a harder person than the one who'd started out on this walk. Jenna went on: 'It's the only way to control this time tunnel. The only way we have any chance of getting home or stopping this time loop.'

'You think we may find another one of your crystals down that hole?' Harper didn't sound as though she thought this was anything of a good idea.

'Miss Tregarthur had one and so did Baylock, who made out he was the head of this family,' I answered, although I didn't see why I should be bothering to persuade her to come with us. 'Baylock lived in the house up there. I don't know if we'll find anything … or anyone. And if we do find anyone, they won't necessarily want to help us. But it is the only place to go.'

'There may be something,' Jenna was trying to be hopeful. It didn't work, none of us felt there was much hope.

We took turns to keep watch throughout the night, although I managed to fall asleep on my shift and didn't wake up until daylight.

'Time to move on,' Jenna stood and pointed to the opening. 'I sort of wondered if we should send Alvin and Mary on their own to explore ahead,' Jenna hid her face and her smile. 'If you do, make sure you get back before tomorrow.'

Jenna was making a point. When we had first been hijacked into another time, Mary and I had disappeared together, going up the mountain trying to find out where we were. We hadn't returned until the next day. I kept saying nothing happened, but Mary had a way to always make it seem worse. Jenna usually found a way to tease me about it, and it always worked.

Jenna was holding out her hand. I handed over a piece of chocolate from my pack, the only way to stop her saying more.

We all set off together. Matt still supporting Stevie. Jack and Mary at the back. Jenna needn't have worried, those two wouldn't be separated. Although Mary still gave me a wink, and Jenna saw me blush.

I hadn't remembered that the path leading from the cave was slippery and wet, and I kept hitting my head. We needed a torch but didn't have one in our packs so we just had to struggle on in the darkness, there was a faint green glow from some of the rocks ahead. Radiation, I remembered. Eventually the tunnel opened out into the cave space we'd slept in so long before.

The green glow was stronger in here. Last time there had been more things in here – a chair, a sort of bed. It had all been smashed, broken pieces of wood. Last time we'd wanted to get out quickly, to return to the moor. I hadn't really noticed that the tunnel went on past the cave.

Demelza pointed it out. 'It's the way to the house, Miss Tregarthur kept looking at it. I think she was scared that some of the other Tregarthurs might appear.'

We went on. The way became easier, the path wider and less damp. There was still no noise even though we kept stopping to listen. The light grew stronger.

The tunnel came to an end in an open space that I remembered. It was made from the rock but more of a room – with beds, a cupboard and other furniture. Now, all smashed.

'We came here before,' Jenna turned. 'After she -' Jenna prodded Demelza hard, 'After she poisoned us.'

Demelza said nothing. I thought I saw a smirk on her face. Demelza might have helped us this time but that didn't mean anything.

This was the place where we'd first met some of Baylock's people. At the time, we had no idea they were all Tregarthurs. They said they had been travelling in time for the good of humanity. I had wanted to believe them, but we didn't have much time for conversation before being attacked.

At the end of this room a huge wooden door with great iron bolts had led to the main house. The cavemen had battered it down to get to us. The door hung open, broken and on rusty hinges. Beyond it, a corridor led into the house. It had been a hallway lined with pictures and ornaments. Pieces from all over time.

Everything that could have been broken had been smashed. Pieces of ancient pots covered the floor. A suit of armour that had stood in a special niche was now broken and bent, it had been thrown into another doorway. Into another completely trashed room.

We stepped over the metal suit and went further down the hall. It was difficult to work out what sort of house this had been. It was certainly very old. But not something from ancient history. The rooms were large, with windows opening onto a yard outside. The wind blew in through the broken glass.

Further on we found the room where we'd met the rest of the 'family'. A room with a fantastic view out over the moor through a huge glass window. The broken glass was spread all over the room, shards all over the remains of the broken table.

The cavemen had taken their revenge here. Cavemen out of their time, in the mess that came with Miss Tregarthur and time travel.

She had used the crystal to do what she wanted, before she died, before she became the tunnel. With her death she could cause all the harm on her own. Before, Miss Tregarthur had no problem with the terrible pain it caused to whatever existed in the stones of the moor. I knew that if we did find another crystal, I wouldn't have any trouble smashing it to pieces if I thought it would hurt that awful person. But I didn't think there was much chance of finding anything in this wrecked house.

We kicked some of the glass out of the way and sat in the long room looking out through the smashed window on to the moor. We could still hear the occasional wail or howl, but no sign of any cavemen as we looked out.

'Any ideas?' asked Jenna.

'About what?' Harper had cut her hand on the glass and was wrapping an army bandage around it, Mary went over and helped. Nurse Mary, as she hated being called.

'Any ideas where they might have kept another crystal?' Jenna went on. 'Maybe Baylock gave us the only other one. It fell apart when I smashed it last time. When the tunnel took us to the time of the war. Miss Tregarthur said we deserved it. We didn't know what she meant until we arrived.'

'But if Baylock, or any of them, had another crystal, where would they have hidden it? If the cavemen found it, they would probably just have thrown it away. It could still be here,' I said, standing up. 'We have to search.'

We spent the day looking and not finding anything. Matt and I went back to look at the cave room's broken door. Although it was smashed we managed to get it back onto the hinges and found some wooden beams to strengthen it. We spent the night in the cave room, it seemed safer to be behind the door. At least we knew there was an escape route. But all was quiet through the night. We didn't sleep much, trying to think of places to search.

In the morning Matt and I went out into the yard. The house stood in a remote part of the moor. Baylock had said few people even knew it was there. There was no road, everything had to be carried or taken on horseback. Standing in the yard and looking back at the house, it was a weird mixture. Some of it looked like houses in our own time, not modern ones, but the posh old red brick houses with the big windows. But another part looked ancient, with a thatched roof that had collapsed. The sort of house that was probably put together over many years – like thousands possibly.

Out in this yard we could see several other buildings. There was a small barn that looked like it had been used for storing firewood, but that had been ruined, as had something that looked like it might have been a hen house.

Another barn seemed to have been used for storing bottles and jars. Perhaps it had been used for brewing or something. The bottles had all been smashed and broken glass was scattered over the ground. Nearly all broken; I saw something.

I turned to Matt, 'You go back and see if the others have found anything. I'll poke around through this stuff. Matt left.

On the floor a bright blue stoppered bottle remained, undamaged. I don't know why I wanted to be on my own. Could this bottle be of any use? I picked it up and brushed away dirt from the label. I could just make out one word, 'cyanide'.

What did Baylock and his family want with cyanide? Maybe this wasn't the place for brewing drink – more a place for brewing up poisons – like the one that Miss Tregarthur had once used on us. Actually, it was Demelza who'd poisoned us, although Demelza had poisoned Miss Tregarthur as well.

Looking around this barn made me wonder if the other Tregarthurs who lived here were as good as they had made out. Maybe they would have poisoned us again if we'd stayed here. This place made me feel uncomfortable, as if someone was watching.

Holding the blue bottle, I shook it but anything in it must have dried out. I took out the stopper and sniffed but there was no smell, not that I knew what cyanide smelt like – I think I was lucky not to find out. I found out later that one sniff can kill you.

I had an idea. Not a very good idea, actually a really bad idea, but at least an idea. I took the bottle. Outside, a half-broken barrel had filled with rain water. I washed out the bottle, several times, before filling it and slipping it into a pocket in my army coat. I went back inside.

At the end of the day we moved back into the room behind the door again. Nobody had found anything else, nothing useful, nothing to eat. Mary had been right, we should have saved some of the food.

'How does Baylock and this family link to the time tunnel?' Jack asked me.

'I think that when they die, they sort of get swallowed up by the moor. They become the time tunnel, or at least they make it work.'

'So it's sort of human?' Harper had been listening to us.

I nodded, 'Maybe.'

'That's what happened to Miss Tregarthur?' Mary had joined us. I nodded again.

'Anyone who died in this house became the tunnel?' Jack said as though he didn't believe it.

'I think it only happened if you were born here as well,' I tried to make a bit more sense of something that clearly didn't make sense at all.

'Who is next?' Jack asked and I didn't answer although I knew who I thought the next person could be.

I woke to another howl. This one was definitely closer. 'We need to leave,' I called to wake the others.

'Nowhere to go,' Jenna moaned.

'Have to take the offer of a trip to America,' Jack looked at Harper.

'Won't happen,' Harper said quietly. 'We'll probably all be shot for desertion.'

'Look up crystal on the mobile,' I said, laughing.

Demelza had held tightly on to the mobile. I think she had tried phoning numbers she remembered, but there was no reply. It was difficult to understand what had happened to everyone in this bubble of the war.

'It says the crystal is in the fireplace,' Demelza said, staring at the mobile screen.

'What? Never?' Jenna rushed over to look, grabbing Demelza.

'Of course it doesn't,' Demelza pulled away, laughing. There was nothing on the screen other than a picture of a dog. Harper's dog.

'Maybe it really is in the fireplace,' Mary stood up and looked at Jack. 'People did hide things in chimney breasts. Hide people too, in priest holes. There's a huge fireplace back in the main house.'

We went back into the big room and searched the massive fireplace. The cavemen howls were getting closer. I kept looking out over the moor. Through the broken window I could see the weather was breaking, the wind getting stronger, black clouds forming.

There was nothing in the chimney.

In the distance, I saw a movement. The cavemen were coming. Perhaps they knew we would make for this house.

'RUN,' I shouted.

We ran back down the devastated hallway, Harper tripping over the armoured suit as she ran, sprawling on the floor. Jenna gave her a hand back up. Then stopped.

Something glowing green fell from the metal hood. Jenna grabbed for it as we heard the first of the cavemen entering the house. The cries they made might not be in a language we understood but the meaning was clear, they were after our blood.

We ran on. Matt and I did our best to shut the door to the tunnel. It wouldn't hold for long.

Then we all ran for it in the dim green light. Matt was still having to pull Stevie along.

This felt like another time loop. We'd done this before. Been chased along this same path by cavemen. How did you know if you were in one of Miss Tregarthur's time loops? Maybe we had been chased down this tunnel over and over again, not realising that time didn't move on.

I wasn't going to find out if letting the cavemen catch us would make it all stop. I ran on. We might be faster runners than them, but they would catch us on the open moor, unless what Jenna had found could save us.

I tripped and fell, scrambled up and ran on. Ahead the light was stronger, behind the howls even louder. Then we were out on the moor. Not far from the Hanging Stones. We'd come out this way before, out through a gap between other stones on the moor.

'I was searching for the entrance,' Jenna said, panting for breath. 'It seems easy now, couldn't find it before.'

'Did you get the crystal, I saw you find something,' Demelza shouted, seeing the cavemen coming out of the tunnel not far behind.

Quickly, Jenna pulled out the small egg-shaped piece of stone, shimmering in the light. We were at the Hanging Stones. I still had Harper's gun and I passed it to Jenna. She stood back and then smashed the barrel of the gun down on the crystal.

The noise was unbearable. It was the howling wail of Miss Tregarthur coming from deep under the Hanging Stones, the terrible noise we'd heard before.

The sound seemed to stop the cavemen, who were jumping around at the tunnel entrance with their hands over their ears.

'Get us home, you bitch,' yelled Jenna, smashing the gun barrel down again. And we waited for the smoke that would signal the opening of the time tunnel.

All that came was a tormented laugh. A noise that seemed to get directly into my head, filling up my mind to the point that it would burst.

The noise changed to words, Miss Tregarthur's words: 'There is nothing you can do. I can survive any pain, I am stronger than you, you will all stay here and die. You thought you could make me take you home. Go on, smash that crystal as hard as you can. I am stronger than that. You will die … die … die.' The sound faded to a hideous laugh.

Jenna pointed the gun at the cavemen and tried to fire, but she must have damaged the mechanism when she struck the crystal, it didn't work. The cavemen were coming, more slowly after the noise, but they were coming.

'No hope,' Jack and Mary held on to each other, in a final embrace.

'At least give me my mobile back,' Harper said to Demelza who shrugged and handed it over.

'You will hear me and obey,' I decided to try a voice like Baylock had once used, as though I was some high priest. Not sure it came out as anything other than a squeak.

Noises from the Hanging Stones seemed to mock me, told me I was useless, told me about my useless family. My dead mother.

I took out the little blue cyanide bottle and removed the stopper.

'You will obey me.' I lifted up the bottle. 'Cyanide. This will kill me. And you know what will happen next.'

I felt the ground shake. Black clouds streamed in above us. The wind screeched to a gale. A roar of anger came from the stones.

'I will do it,' I shouted.

'No,' cried Jenna as I lifted the bottle to my lips and took a sip hoping I'd washed it clean enough.

'One more drop and I will die,' I called out. 'Then you will be gone. Then *I* will control time, your time will be over. I am from the family, I was born in the house, I am next. When I die, I will chase you from the moor for ever. I will be the one, you have no choice.'

The roaring howl broke to a sob, all the force draining from Miss Tregarthur.

'Take us back in time to the beginning, back to the cave, back to my injured mother, take us NOW.'

A choking smoke rose from the Hanging Stones. I beckoned the others to run into it, but held my hand up to stop Harper. 'If you try to follow us, I think you will die.'

Harper took another step and it was as if an electric shock took her, she shot backwards. The tunnel would never take someone from the present time, it never had, we had lost the baby Zog, we had lost Kan with Posy, and we were going to lose Harper.

'It's ok,' she said, looking up; three helicopters whirled in the air, dropping exploding gas canisters on the cavemen. 'I used the mobile.'

I laughed, making for the smoke of time.

'I'm staying,' Demelza pulled away from Jenna.

10

TROUBLE IN TIME

We whirled into the spiral of time. All I could hear was her laugh. Why should Miss Tregarthur laugh? Hadn't I broken her? My threat to take the poison remained. If she did not take us back to the cave with my mother, then I could still take away her power, replace her in the stones of the moor. Had she seen through my plan? Did she know that there was nothing poisonous in the bottle I used? Maybe I had to find a more convincing way to die.

It wasn't a great idea, but what other choice did I have? If I could take her place, at least I could try to sort out the mess she had made. It was so bizarre that Miss Tregarthur had been trying to kill me over and over again, and now she needed me to stay alive.

We arrived with a bump onto ... what?

'Where are we?' I think all of us said the same thing at the same time.

Matt and Stevie looked the most confused. They still hadn't recovered from the war. I didn't think they'd ever recover, unless maybe we sorted this out and managed to get them home. Perhaps then their memories would be different. If we could alter the mess Miss Tregarthur had made, then the war might never have happened. But it had, we'd been there, Ryan had been shot. Surely we couldn't unmake all that? But we had to try.

I looked around. We were high up, but something was very wrong. I couldn't make out what was not right, but I had been to this place before, been here with Mary, not long after we had first travelled in time.

We were in front of the Hanging Stones, but in their giant form before thousands of years had worn them down. The thousands of years we had been taken back in time. Around us the ground sloped away. Mary and I had made our way up here to the top of this vast hill, searching for answers that we never found, only more unanswerable questions.

'Alvin,' Mary's voice gave away that she obviously recognised where we were.

'Ah,' said Jenna and I waited for trouble. 'This is the place you two came to for your night of passion.'

'It wasn't like that,' Mary and I said together.

'Of course it wasn't,' Jenna hopefully was being sarcastic.

'There was a storm,' Mary went on quickly: 'We found the writing, Miss Tregarthur's writing, her notebook, where she explained the promise to her father.'

'Ah,' said Jenna.

'It must have been around here,' Mary said.

'Look,' I ran forward and pointed. 'The tin, isn't that the tin of dog food?'

'Dog food?' shouted all the others together.

'Miss Tregarthur's dog,' Mary said. 'We found the tin along with her notebook. And we ...'

'Ate the lot,' I said remembering how good it was to have anything to eat – even if we didn't know what was in a tin of dog food.

I looked down at the empty rusting tin. I could just make out the remains of the doggy picture on the side.

'Whatever happened to Miss Tregarthur's dog - Smut, wasn't it?' I said, not thinking anyone would know.

'We saw Smut, in the nursing home,' Mary explained. 'Miss Tregarthur was injured in the first earthquake, she never came with us. We found her in a nursing home. She seemed to be in a coma. The dog was with her.'

'Miss Tregarthur soon recovered all of her nasty self,' I said.

'But I don't think her dog was likely to survive. He could hardly get out of his basket, even though he gave us a growl,' Jack added.

The only sense I could make of that was that Miss Tregarthur must have pretended to be injured, pretended to be in a coma, just waiting to cause the mess she had done.

I bent down to pick up the tin. I couldn't move it. 'Stuck,' I said, tugging away at the metal. I gave it a kick, nothing happened. My foot just glided past.

'There's something very strange about this place.' Jenna walked away to the edge of the hill. She waved to us to follow.

Had she seen the mammoths? Mary and I had seen mammoths the first time we came here. That was when we knew we had come back in time. That was when we realised how much trouble we were in. We walked over to join Jenna, who was pointing down to the bottom of the hill, and she wasn't speaking.

'Mammoths,' I said. 'We saw them before.'

'But ...' Mary stopped, realising that it wasn't just the ancient mammoths that were strange.

'They aren't moving.' Mary looked around. 'Nothing is moving.'

And she was right. Several mammoths must have wandered out of the wood, far below, but they weren't wandering now, they had stopped in mid step. Nothing moved. Nothing. There was no wind, and when I looked up, the clouds weren't moving.

Matt had sat down on the grass, holding his head, 'It's not real,' he moaned. 'Look at this.' He poked at a tuft of grass. It didn't move.

'No sounds,' Stevie had joined Matt.

Wherever and whenever we had arrived, we were not really part of this world. Nothing moved and we couldn't move anything. Walking over the ground it felt as though we were above it, even though I could see the grass beneath my feet.

'Miss T's beaten us,' I shouted into the non-existent wind. 'Every turn we make, she fixes it so we can't escape.'

I suppose my miserable voice infected the others. We ended up sitting on the ground, that wasn't the ground, or whatever. What time were we in? We were on the top of this strange hill, a dome shape that Mary had said looked like a cake – we were so hungry at the time that everything looked like uneatable food.

Eventually Jenna stood up again, 'We need to get down to the bottom of this hill.' She turned to Mary. 'You and Alvin came back down to us, in the end, how?'

Mary got up and pointed. 'There's a path, over there. You're not going to like it.'

I gave another groan, but Jenna poked me and pulled my arm, so we all moved.

As we walked in the direction that Mary had pointed it became clear that there was a huge hollow in this hill top. Getting nearer the hollow became a hole, nearer still and it was an abyss.

'That's big,' Matt said, looking down. 'You could get a load of mammoths into a hole like that.'

'Hundreds,' Stevie suddenly added in a squeaky voice.

I looked at the two of them. They reminded me what it was like when we were all at school, squeaky voiced teenagers coming up with teenage thoughts. A lot had happened since then, very little for the better.

'There's a path, somewhere,' I said, not exactly wanting to find it. It made me dizzy just staring down into the hole.

'Here,' Mary had already started to lower herself over the edge onto the narrow track. 'Come on.'

This was where Mary and I had sheltered from a storm. Sheltered through the night, clinging on to the rocks, feeling the tremors from earthquakes that had threatened to send us tumbling down to our deaths. At least *I* was clinging to the rocks, Mary had been clinging to me and I hoped that she wasn't going to say anything more about that.

This time with Mary going first it seemed to make everyone braver. And slowly we made our way down the dangerous, steep path. Last time it had been slippery from the drenching rain. This time it didn't really feel like anything. Before there had been huge rocks blocking our way. This time there was nothing to stop us. It felt too easy, I wondered what we were going to find. We reached the bottom.

'Through there,' Mary made for a dark opening in the rock. 'Quick.'

To get from the bottom of the hole, Mary and I had crawled through yet another tunnel to get back to the rest of the school hiking group. Finding Miss Tregarthur's notebook, seeing the mammoths, meant we were coming back to tell the rest of them that we really had travelled in time. The start of this hellish nightmare.

I felt Mary was right to hurry, we had to get out of here in case of more earthquakes. Even if we might not feel part of this world, it felt as though things could change at any moment. We crawled as fast as we could, but in silence. The touch of the rock strangely smooth, as though there was a layer between it and us.

Coming back out into daylight on the other side we felt relief, but felt at the complete mercy of Miss Tregarthur, and she hadn't shown any mercy to anyone.

'The river,' Jack shouted.

We'd all been here together. Miss Tregarthur's first hike had brought us through an earthquake and through time to reach this ancient world. The river had been a crashing torrent, smashing through boulders; a river that formed a barrier. A barrier that had kept us locked in the place we had arrived, until we eventually found a way to cross.

It wasn't real. The river had stopped, crests of spray topped rapids held in mid-air. There was no sound from the water, no movement.

I looked up. The hill rose above us, a steep rocky cliff on this side.

I just knew this was going to get worse. 'Come on,' I said, searching for a way though the bushes that covered the ground at the bottom of the cliff. 'We have to find the … cave.'

I pushed on with so many thoughts in my head. Why had there been so many caves and tunnels? Was this because Miss Tregarthur was part of the rock, all of this seemed to come from the rocks of the moor. The stones that seemed timeless themselves but controlled time for others.

We found a path, overgrown but still a path. We seemed to glide through. The bushes didn't move, they just weren't there as we went to push them aside. I hurried on, still registering that finding a path wasn't necessarily a good thing. Who had made the path?

Soon we would be back at the cave, the place where all this had started. When all our group had plummeted though time, snatched away into Miss Tregarthur's promise to her dead father. Her plan for us to become part of the caveman world, a genetic plan to provide children for a race that was dying.

Most of our group appeared to escape, back into the time tunnel. But in a crazy mad way, Jenna and I had decided to stay. Somehow, we had felt we could make a better life here in this world rather than face all our trouble at home. That was never to be. In no way had we understood the terrible power Miss Tregarthur wielded. We were set upon, caught in the middle of a battle between two tribes of cave people, driven on by the person we thought was dead – Zach. The school bully who became Miss Tregarthur's murderous pawn.

And through the middle of this battle, in another bizarre twist, my mother had appeared. She had been snared in Miss Tregarthur's schemes. She was trying to save us in the battle, but she had suffered terrible wounds. I was sure I saw her die. At that moment, the time tunnel had opened once more, we could escape - or so we had thought - and we took our chance, leaving Mum's dead body on the cave floor.

It would never be that easy.

For a start, we didn't escape and ended up in a village dying of the Black Death, and, just as bad, Jenna had once confessed that she saw a flicker in my mother's eyes as we fled. But Jenna was unsure, she had felt it was unlikely that Mum could have survived. I had seen the gaping wound in her side, no one could have lived after that, could they?

Now we were back, would I find out the truth about Mum? But it would be Miss Tregarthur's truth, and probably not the real truth. I could see the cave ahead. I started to run. I had to see. Mum had been in my thoughts for so long. My family had fallen apart. Nothing could keep Mum and Dad together. Dad and my brother had finally been caught and sent to jail. Could I save Mum, get her back to our real time? Could I even hope to think we could have a home? Once more?

I stopped outside the cave, frightened to look, to go on. Matt went on ahead with Jack. I started to follow. Suddenly Jack turned and held up his hands, 'Stop.'

I tried to brush him aside. 'Let me through.'

'NO,' Jack shouted. 'It's a trap. This is the reason she sent us here.'

I could see into the cave behind Jack. There we were. It was like the last time, when the battling cavemen and more of the people we knew had been there. What I could see was a frozen scene. Mum lay on the cave floor but it was only Jenna and me beside her, no one else. I could see myself, another Alvin. No one was moving, this was some sort of time warp that Miss Tregarthur had made. We were frozen in time along with Mum. I needed to get in there, to push past Jack.

'It's a trap,' Jack shouted again, grabbing my arm.

'What're you talking about?' Again, I tried to shove him out of the way.

'It's a time thing.' Jack had been joined by Mary, the others stood to one side. I looked at Jenna, who just shrugged. We didn't understand.

'You are in the cave and you are outside, the same you.' Jack was trying to put words together and I wasn't sure whether to believe him, but he had got most things right before, so I let him go on. 'I think if you meet yourself then something really bad could happen, something Miss Tregarthur could have dreamt up. You can't meet yourself, you'll die.'

'But if it kills me, then she will have lost, I'll get sucked into the stones like she did,' I said. 'That can't be her plan.'

'That won't happen if this is her plan,' Mary joined in. 'What if the two of you meet and cancel each other out? Sounds like the sort of thing that could happen in time travel. I don't know, but why don't you let us go in first?'

'And if that did happen, then you and your mum would vanish, leaving Miss Tregarthur the only controller of time,' Jack spoke quickly, rushing his words, sounding frantic.

'You can't let that happen,' Stevie seemed to have picked up Jack's fears. 'Please Alvin. Think of that war, you can't let it go on.' Stevie clung on to Matt, shouting: 'Don't let him.'

I could see this was so much more than worrying about their own survival. They had seen more of the war in those trenches, so many deaths, a war without end.

But could I watch Mum die again? Was that what Miss Tregarthur wanted, to torment me, stuck in an unreal time, forever to watch Mum in this cave? Was there no way out?

'I have to get Mum into the time tunnel, back home, stop

her dying,' I cried.

'I don't think Miss Tregarthur would let that happen, even if you threaten to poison yourself again.' Mary held on to me.

'It wasn't real,' I said. 'The poison wasn't real.'

'We know,' Jenna smiled.

'Let us try first.' Jack turned towards the cave.

I looked at Jenna, who gave me a 'who knows' look.

'Make it quick.' I waved Jack and Mary forward.

The frozen scene in the cave seemed to be in its own bubble, as though there was something physical between them and us standing outside. As the two of them approached the air appeared to stretch, bugling inwards as they went forward.

'Alvin, Jenna. Keep away, keep out of sight,' Mary called. 'Don't try and come in, even if you see your mother move.'

'I'll try,' I mumbled. This was hard. I had so many confused ideas about my family, where we had come from, why Mum was ever involved with the Tregarthurs? I wasn't going to leave Jack and Mary alone for too long. I felt Jenna beside me, holding my arm. She'd know there was a chance I would just charge into the cave – I don't think she'd be able to stop me.

'Come away, at least a bit,' Jenna said quietly.

'Can't,' I shrugged away, but she grabbed hold of me again and she gave Matt a nod.

Jack and Mary were in the cave. I could see myself and the other Jenna. I could feel it. I felt dragged towards them. I could see Jenna felt the same. Whatever was dragging us into the cave was getting stronger.

Jack and Mary were talking. I saw Mum move, injured but making frantic weak gestures. I couldn't hear the words, this was taking forever. I had to go to her.

Mary ran out. 'Alvin, get away,' she shouted. 'You're both getting dragged towards each other. Time is trying to do it, you can't be here with your other self.'

'Get away,' came a scream from inside the cave. Mum. She must be alive. I had to go to her.

'NO,' Mary shoved me. 'You must do what she says. Do what your mum says. Matt, help.'

They were right, I felt the pull, some force dragging me back to the cave. We tried to fight it. Matt, Stevie and Mary held us, pulled us. The force became weaker as we moved away, out of sight.

Mary tried to explain. 'Your mum says that everything will collapse if you meet up with your other self.'

'How does she know that?' I asked. Mum couldn't have left the cave, couldn't have spoken to anyone, how did she know what might happen?

'Miss Tregarthur has kept her trapped in this time bubble,' Mary said. 'And she has loaded the pain on to your mum, told her the plan to kill you all by getting the different versions of yourself to meet.'

'But Miss Tregarthur is dead, how could she talk to Mum?'

'This is the very start, right here.' Mary was still pushing me away from the cave. 'This is the place and the time when it all started. This is the furthest back in history that any one of them could go.'

'But ...' I started, I had no idea what to say next.

Mary went on: 'You know there was a tunnel at the back of the cave, it's how the others got home. It's right underneath the Hanging Stones up on the hill. It's the stones that connect them, the link. Miss Tregarthur should be dead but the worst part of her lives on in the stones, all the way through time. She has haunted your mum, still is haunting her.'

'Bbb ... but ... that's not right ... have to be younger ... how?' I burbled words that made no sense.

'I don't think there is any sense in this,' Mary said and I could see she was finding it hard to hold herself together. 'Your mum says Miss Tregarthur has so much hate that she will destroy us all. She says you must keep away. Can you do that? I need to get back to Jack, I think there is a lot more that has to be done, more to make us all safe. To make your mum safe.'

'No.' I tried to push past Matt. I knew what Mary meant. It could only mean one thing. I couldn't let this happen.

Jenna held me tight. She realised the same. 'It's the only way. You have to let them do it.'

I felt my anger drain away. Jenna had done this before. Only Jenna could have stopped me charging back into the cave. But she did stop me.

'Come on.' Jenna pulled at me.

'Where?' I choked.

'Let's do something cheerful – like look at the graves.' Jenna gave me a shove, I stumbled and we ended up walking down the slope towards the place we had found the grave of Miss Tregarthur's father. And the place we had buried Susie, the girl who had died so soon after we had arrived here, the first time.

Mary had returned to the cave.

I walked on with Jenna as though in a trance. As we walked away I felt the pull of the cave disappear, the physical pull might have gone, but the wrench in my mind didn't. Would I just have to leave the last few minutes of my mother's life to someone else? It might still be an Alvin, but not the same

Alvin that I was living in at that moment. How did that work? Maybe both Alvins were thinking the same. What was the other Alvin? Where had this one come from? Completely confused I stumbled on.

'I'd forgotten about Trog.' Jenna pointed at the crude gravestones we had made at the time, and she walked forward to brush away the plants that had grown over them. She couldn't do it. We still weren't really part of this world.

I looked at the stone. 'Trog' was the name we'd given to the cavewoman we had met. She had appeared with her baby – Zog. Trog had been killed by Zach, his first taste of death in his change from school bully to Miss Tregarthur's pet monster.

We sat on the ground, it might have been wet but we felt no dampness. Jenna kept trying to talk about the things that had happened here. How we had been so near to death, all the terrible things that Miss Tregarthur and her promise had brought upon us. I heard the sound of Jenna's words but couldn't concentrate on their meaning. I was in my own bubble, imagining the things that might have been.

It was probably only a few minutes, but it might have been another thousand years, before Jack and Mary came back. They stood for a moment looking at the graves.

I wanted answers, I wanted to shout for answers. But I didn't, because I thought I knew what they were going to say.

11

THE ONLY WAY

'It can't be,' I said. The others were pretty much holding me down, stopping me from charging up to the cave.

'It's what your mum says,' Mary said in her gentlest voice.

'What does it matter if I go to Mum?' I pointed up the hill. 'What does it matter if I explode in some bomb of time?'

'It won't just be you.' I could tell that Jack felt this was obvious, the explanation he gave made perfect sense to him.

'It won't just be you,' Jack repeated. 'If you meet up with your other selves, Jenna will die as well. What happens may be so strong that we all die.'

'Even if we don't die, we will be stuck here forever.' Mary had her hand on my shoulder.

'Or back in that war,' Stevie said with a wide-eyed stare.

'Tell me again,' I said. 'I didn't get it the first time.' I relaxed for a moment. I think the others were suspicious that I would jump up if they let me go, so they all stayed close. I wasn't a good enough person to believe that it would be the thought of the war that would have stopped me. But when Mary said it would be Jenna's death as well, that stopped me. I couldn't let more harm come to Jenna. We had been through so much together.

'But is Mum dead now?' I asked, confused.

'No … not really … no,' Jack didn't sound certain.

'When we came back out of the cave,' Mary tried to be more definite. 'It's as though everything in there all goes back to being frozen. We stood outside and looked back in. There's no change.' She turned to Jack.

'The three of them in that cave stop moving,' Jack explained. 'It's as though it's just waiting for you and Jenna. Miss Tregarthur has set this up.'

'Ok,' I said and repeated: 'Tell me again. Tell me why there is only one way, and why Mum has to die?'

Jack and Mary took turns to go back over what had happened in the cave.

Mary started: 'The reason this will work is that Miss Tregarthur doesn't know that your mother was born in Baylock's house.'

'She knows Alvin was born there, but didn't know about his mum.' Jack went on to explain to Matt and Stevie why that was important.

We had learnt this before. Being born in that house brought a terrible burden. It meant that if you died near to the Hanging Stones, near to where the time tunnel appeared, then you would be swallowed up into the rocks of the moor. We had seen it happen, that weird formation, appearing as two balanced stones, which were actually just one until the death happened. Then it broke apart, forming a pincer, which had dragged away the body of Miss Tregarthur. She had become the spirit in the time tunnel, and her vengeful spirit would not rest, it sought our deaths.

Before she had died it was so different. Then she had wanted me to die first, for me to be swallowed up into the stones of the moor. She believed that I would be easy to control with her crystal, forcing me to take her wherever she wanted in time. Striking the crystal brought such terrible pain to the tunnel that it would do anything she wanted. Once it had been her own sister, the spirit in the tunnel before. Miss Tregarthur didn't seem to mind who she hurt to get her own way.

And she had overcome the force of the crystal, perhaps she was too evil to mind the pain. Even my threat of death had been ineffective. Miss Tregarthur wanted to return us to this time and this place. I just fell for it. She must have known that when we met our alternative selves in time we would cancel each other out. She must have known that I would disappear and not replace her in the tunnel. Probably Jack was right – the force of our meeting wouldn't just cancel me out, it would wipe out Jenna and my mum as well.

After Baylock's house and his family had been destroyed it was unlikely that anyone else would be born there. The threat to replace Miss Tregarthur would be gone, her spirit would live on for ever. She had found her own eternity, with no one to take her place.

Were Jack and Mary right? Did Miss Tregarthur really not know my mother had been born in the house? Wouldn't Baylock have told her? Was there something else?

'Miss Tregarthur wouldn't have known that your grandmother came to the house,' Mary slowed in her explanation. 'She came as a servant and ...' Mary stopped.

'And ...' I asked realising the truth.

'Yes, she got pregnant by Baylock.' Jack didn't seem as worried about the effect this would have on me. He was right, I had expected something like this. But maybe it could explain why

Baylock didn't tell everyone, maybe Miss Tregarthur didn't know that Mum could …

'Hang on!' I almost jumped up, feeling several hands grabbing me. 'Wasn't Baylock born there himself? Isn't he the next one for the tunnel? Actually, why isn't he in the tunnel now? I'm pretty sure the cavemen must have killed him.'

'Apparently, he wasn't born there, he just found the place,' Mary said. 'But I think there might be more to his story than we know.'

'What about the other two of Miss Tregarthur's relatives?' I said. 'Her so-called step-brother or nephew or whatever that man Hugh said he was.'

'Demelza said they weren't real family.' Mary had, apparently, got more information from Demelza.

I wasn't sure this all added up. It seemed more likely that Miss Tregarthur had kept mum alive, to stop her taking her place in the time tunnel. If Jack and Mary were right and both mum and I disappeared in some strange conflict of time, then there would be no chance of ever replacing Miss Tregarthur. But if Mum's plan worked then it could mean the absolute end of that terrible woman.

I realised that we were in silence, surrounded by the graves. Just some of the deaths this whole thing had caused. None of the others said anything more. They were waiting for me. I wasn't sure I could cope with sentencing Mum to life in the rocks of the moor. Life in the moor until … until I died. I asked them to repeat everything again, hoping that wasn't the only way.

'So, you want to drag Mum into the back of the cave, into the tunnel?' I stared at the ground. 'You want her to die and that will make it all right? Well it won't.' I buried my head in my hands.

'It's not us that want it …' Jack blurted and would have said more except Mary slapped her hand over his mouth. 'What?' he spluttered.

'No, it's not you, of course, it's not you. You can blame my Mum, can't you? You can say it was all her idea to die and live on in that time thing,' I said, feeling every part of me hating the idea.

'It can't be her. It's you that want it. You say there is no other way, there must be another way. There has to be another way,' I broke down and Jenna pushed the others away and held me. I knew it wasn't them. I knew this plan had come from my mother. And I knew it was the only way.

'You're just going to drag her into the back and dump her, or what?' I asked after more useless argument about other non-existent ideas.

'No … of course we won't dump her … we'll carry her and …' I could hear Mary trying to be gentle but none of us knew what would happen.

We'd been there when Miss Tregarthur had died and been swallowed into the rocks. It hadn't been gentle at all. A raging storm mixed with earth tremors, lightning bolts and the moor had wrenched apart to take her body.

Would this be different? So many things seemed so difficult, 'Is there even a tunnel at the back of the cave?' I asked. 'I mean, last time we had to clear out the tunnel – you remember Jack? It took days and then after you'd left, it all collapsed, the tunnel was completely closed off.'

'We have to hope it works, we can't …' Jack stopped. I realised what he was going to say.

'We can't take her up to the Hanging Stones, can't drag … or

113

carry ... her up that path. She's too weak for that,' I said. 'If it doesn't work then Mum dies and it will have all been useless.' I was trying to remember if there had been any part of the tunnel left last time. It was impossible because we didn't know if this was like 'last time' or if it was something different that Miss Tregarthur had made happen.

'We can't tell,' Jack said. 'We can't tell if there is any tunnel, we can't tell if it will work.'

'We're all going to die,' Stevie moaned. 'Nothing will work. That Miss Tregarthur, she's way ahead of us, something will go wrong.' He sank to the ground and went on moaning.

We hadn't taken much notice of Stevie. We all knew he was in a mess after the war and hadn't any idea how to help him. Matt seemed to do his best, but that was just physical, picking him up and moving him on. I wanted to believe that if we got him home he would be better, but I had the awful feeling that he was right. We'd never beaten Miss Tregarthur before, not really.

'Stevie,' Mary put her hand on his shoulder. 'You may be right, but I think this really is the only way, the only chance we have.'

'Can't you go in and check out the cave? See if there is any sign of the time tunnel?' I asked.

'It's a bubble,' Jack explained. 'Your mum told us to keep away. If we burst through then your Mum thinks that time sort of starts from then, she will only have a few minutes left for us to move her.'

I had a sudden thought, 'What does Alvin say? What does the other Alvin say?'

'And the other Jenna,' said the Jenna standing next to me.

'Nothing,' said Jack. 'It's not like they are real. I don't know what they are. I don't know what will happen if we do burst through to your mum.'

We needed to move, but they were still waiting for me to take a lead, to tell them to go to the cave, none of them wanted to start this unless I made it happen. But I couldn't.

I was just staring into space, hoping something would happen so that we didn't have to do this. Staring into space and watching clouds. They hadn't moved since we arrived. This wasn't real time.

I looked again. The clouds weren't moving but was I crazy? They were changing colour, changing through dark to black. That could only mean that Miss Tregarthur was working out our idea. It had to be her, she was doing this. The sky was a gathering force of anger. She had to have guessed our plans. Could we do anything before she stopped us?

'We have to do it now,' Jenna pointed at the sky.

'GO,' I shouted to the others.

Jack, Mary and Matt rushed back up to the cave. Stevie stayed where he was on the ground. I saw them stand talking for a while. Then Jack gave a signal and the three of them charged in. I couldn't see what happened. There was a sound like rushing water, a gust of wind blew past us, as though new air was being sucked in to the cave.

Seconds later Mary rushed out, 'Alvin, come, NOW,' and she disappeared.

I ran. Jenna followed. Stevie came more slowly. I guess we all expected the worst.

In the cave, Jack and Matt were lifting my mother's body,

carrying it to the back of the cave. There was just enough light to see that an opening had formed but after a few feet it looked blocked by fallen rocks.

I was the only Alvin, Jenna was the only Jenna.

'As soon as we broke in the others disappeared,' Mary panted.

'Wait,' I called to Jack. 'Wait for me.' I leapt towards them. 'Stop,' I shouted.

'NO, don't stop,' I heard my mother gasp.

We all moved together with my calling, 'Mum, Mum', and my feeling a hot flush of tears on my face.

Jack and Matt laid Mum on the ground. It was the furthest they could go. They stood back, leaving me kneeling on the ground.

'Mum.'

'I'm sorry Alvin, sorry for …' Her face screwed up with pain. 'Sorry.'

'It's alright Mum,' I didn't know why I said that, nothing was alright.

Mum stirred again, 'You have to do what I said before. It won't be over until you get them all back, all who are alive in the wrong times, I will help but you must search for them.' Her hand jerked out, grabbing my arm. 'You must.' I saw the effort this movement had taken.

'But aren't there others we don't know about?' I was sure that Baylock had said there were others, not just us messing about in time.

'They're all dead,' Mum whispered. 'All dead, her fault, Alice Tregarthur's fault.'

'But … Mum.'

'Now you must leave me.' I had to lean right over her to

hear the words.

'No, never,' I felt my voice crack.

'Go, you must go or time will take you as well.'

I'd never had much of a physical closeness to Mum before, none of our family had that closeness. But I bent forward and kissed her cheek, even that hurt her.

'Go,' the words croaked out, her last words. I stood.

The first lightning bolt crashed into the cliff, there was an explosion of light in the cave, followed by the crash of thunder strong enough to shake me to the ground.

'Alvin,' I heard Jenna shriek.

I stepped away from Mum's body, but I couldn't leave her.

The others were shouting but I couldn't hear their words. They were at the entrance to the cave. Shouting for me to come before they left. Even in that moment I saw Jenna grab something. I couldn't see what, why had she done that, it seemed to stick in my mind. Something was holding me back, stopping me from running.

The storm raged. Bolts of lightning smashed down into the ground, into the trees, the noise of thunder blotted out all other sounds. The cave was starting to crumble, rocks falling from the roof.

Matt was there, just like the last time in the trenches, he picked me up, threw me over his shoulder and charged out of the cave.

I looked back. Mum had disappeared, buried under a landslide.

We tumbled outside, crashing into the rest of them, Jenna grabbing me and pulling me away. I ran.

The world had become alive for us. All around us boulders

crashed down from the cliff, thundering down the hill. I felt the pain as something hit me. But I didn't stop, we ran on. Soon we were amongst thick bushes. Lightning was firing into the trees, bringing them down, we ran faster. We had to get away, the whole cliff was falling.

A noise, louder than even the thunder, blasted out through the storm. A screaming howl of anger, the terrible sound of Miss Tregarthur, her wish to defy time, to live on in the tunnel forever. It felt as though she still would win, she would not be defeated.

But even louder I heard the roar of Mum's voice: 'Alice, you are finished, this is your end.' The sound echoed through me. With one last howl, Miss Tregarthur's voice died in the wind. This was the time for my mother. She became the spirit in the stones, the one to control time. Mum was dead, but alive for ever.

I had no time to grieve her death. The whole hill collapsed behind us in a spreading avalanche of rubble. We had to run for our lives, further and further. Tumbling rocks were crashing into trees all around us.

'Make for the river,' I shouted, but not really having any idea where that might be. It seemed to take for ever but we burst out into the open, the river in front of us. We would have reached the river whichever way we'd taken, it curved around, the river that had trapped us before. We were back in this world and the river ran again. Cascades of spray splashing out as the rocks fell. We could watch it happening. Panting for breath we stopped and turned to look back.

'Look,' Jenna pointed. 'The stones.'

In the mass of falling rock the Hanging Stones came down

from the top of the huge hill that had stood above the cave. The Hanging Stones slid in slow motion, riding this vast avalanche.

The landslide stopped. A mound of crushed stone stood where there had once been a huge hill. The thunderous noise echoed back from the mountains in the distance. Then there was silence. The gigantic forces of nature had finished. But not all the rocks had broken.

On top of the mound of rubble one rock, stood out. The Hanging Stone, one rock in a cloud of dust.

12

THE SEARCH BEGINS

'It's real.' Jenna had bent down at the river's edge, with water running over her hand. 'It's real, you can touch things, change things.' Jenna pulled up a handful of grass.

'I think time started for us as soon as we burst the bubble in the cave,' Jack said, looking into the distance. 'Like it kick-started and we are back into some form of whatever is real.'

I was looking up at the strange stone – the Hanging Stone as we've always called it.

'What now? Mum said we had to get everyone back.' I made my voice as firm as I could. We didn't need me to collapse in a weepy fit.

'I hope she's going to help us, now she's gone,' said Mary, probably not realising what she'd said.

I collapsed in a weepy fit.

'Where do we start?' Jenna pulled me to her.

It took a while for me to get my mind back together.

'I guess we have to go back to all the places where we left people, that's what Mum said. I looked at Jack, people had been asking me questions ever since we'd started out on this trip. I hoped someone else might answer them.

'Did you leave anyone here in this time?' Jack asked. 'In this caveman time? I know most of us went back home, at least for a while. Didn't Sam and Ivy stay here?'

'But, we met up with them again and ...' I didn't want to tell Jack about Ivy and Sam yet, maybe we would see them again, I could imagine that was going to cause problems – or at least one very big problem.

'So, there isn't anyone left here?' Jack asked again.

'Only the dead,' Jenna answered. 'Sorry Alvin, but apart from your mother there was Susie who died after eating the chuckerns, and Miss Tregarthur's father. They are in the graves.' Jenna pointed back towards the mound of rocks. The gravesite had been covered over in rubble from the hill. But this wasn't the only place we had buried people who had been taken away on Miss Tregarthur's walk in time.

'There's another grave still in this time.' I turned away.

'Another grave?' said Jack.

'There was another grave. I was taken to it by the cavemen.' I was going to say it seemed so long ago, but that would have been a really stupid thing to say, especially since it might have been quite recently, not a few thousand years ago.

'David told me it was my mother's grave, he lied to me,' I said, and started chucking stones into the river, it seemed to be the thing I'd taken to doing when I got angry, better I suppose than killing people.

'David?' Jack frowned. 'Oh yes, he was meant to be Miss Tregarthur's brother, wasn't he?'

'Maybe, but maybe not.' I looked at the Hanging Stones on the mound of rock, would I hear my mum speak if I went up to them? Would she tell me who David really was? We had found him, held captive by a group of cavemen. We found him and heard so many lies; lies about his relationship with my mum, how they'd travelled in time together; how mum had died trying to escape – who was supposed to have killed her? He showed me a grave – said it was Mum. All lies, but if it wasn't Mum's grave then who was under that mound of earth?

'Wasn't David killed by the cavemen?' Stevie said. 'That's what you told us? I remember you telling us about it. When you came back, when …' His voice trailed off as he remembered all the things that had happened.

David was a key to Miss Tregarthur's hatred. She had made a promise to save him and failed. I had watched the cavemen club David to death – hadn't I? Miss Tregarthur had blamed me. But how could I be sure that he had died? My mother hadn't been dead, even if she was being kept alive in a time bubble trap. Had the man David died? Jenna was staring at me. I knew what that meant.

'If Mum says … if Mum said.' I stopped, was she dead? How could she be dead and still be alive in the time tunnel?

'If Mum said we have to take everyone back, then we have to start here and check.' I looked round our small group. There had been many more of us who had first set off with Miss Tregarthur. I hoped they were safe, but they might be trapped in Miss Tregarthur's war.

'We'll have to go out to the place where we met David, to make sure,' I said that and it felt just like the first time, when I had said we had to set out on another rescue expedition. That had been the first time I had taken charge, something I would never have done before. I was not that sort of person back at school. Me and my family were dangerous. At least Dad was, and it seemed to fit that Mum had to escape. I just didn't imagine her escape would be to thousands of years into the past. It hadn't done her any good in the end and it still didn't explain David, or who was in that other grave.

The problem with taking charge once, they all assumed what I said would keep happening. Jack and Mary were already talking about getting food to take, telling Matt and Stevie what to collect. Jenna was smiling, she must have thought this was as weird as I did.

'Hang on,' I said. 'I think just Matt should come with me. We'll be faster and with just two of us we might avoid the cavemen.'

That soon set the rest arguing, just as it had before. Arguing who should go, when no one would really want to set out into this dangerous world, or dangerous time. But in the end, it was agreed and I left with Matt the next morning, after a breakfast of berries. Our time here had at least taught us which fruits were safe to eat. We left the others behind to find more food and wait.

'Chuckerns are back,' I called, seeing a flock of the strange birds coming into land.

This time we didn't have to cross over a fallen tree to get over the river. The landslide meant we could find our way over fallen rocks and soon we were on the grassy plain. Once we had hunted here, this time we went as quickly as we could. I suppose my life on the sailing boats, and Matt's in the war trenches, had made us much fitter than we had been when we set off from school on Miss Tregarthur's hike. We soon reached the forest, searching for the track that would lead us back to where we had first met the caveman – trying to forget anything about sabre tooth tigers. The day was ending as we reached the top of the hill, looking down on what had been the cavemen's village of huts. There was nothing to see, no cavemen. If any of them had survived they must have moved on.

'What's that?' Matt pointed.

A trail of smoke rose from another part of the valley below.

'We'll wait until morning,' I said, stretching out on the ground. 'If there's any chance it might be David, I don't want to meet him in the dark.'

At least it wasn't a cold night and there were no storms, this time. That had to be unusual for the moor. I could have done with something other than berries to eat though, berries carried in our pockets and squashed.

In the earliest of lights, we made our way down towards where the smoke had come from. Last time we'd tried to creep up on the cavemen it had been useless. They had silently surrounded us as soon as we reached the bottom. No one appeared this time.

'Whatever time this is,' I said, 'it can't be that long after we were here before.'

There were still some signs of where the village had been; broken huts, bones which must have come from the mammoth we had seen killed. There were still some of the creeper ropes that had once made a bridge across the ravine, the bridge that had collapsed killing so many of the cavemen.

We could see a track running down to the river below. And more smoke. We moved on slowly, stopping behind each bush.

'Wh…' Matt smothered a screech. He pointed. Next to him was a stake, and on top the partly decayed head of a caveman.

'Must be something to keep people away,' I looked ahead

124

and could see more heads set out along the path. We crept on. We heard voices. I motioned for us to climb silently up from the track, to get a better view.

'David,' I whispered.

Below us was another hut, better made than the ones the cavemen had lived in. David had been busy, he must have made more cooking pots, brought a stream of water to the hut by partly damming the river, and all around were the heads on stakes.

David was not alone; two cavewomen were doing all the work. David was still hobbling on his stick. I was never sure how he had really hurt his leg. He'd said it was trying to save Mum, or some other lie. His leg didn't seem to be getting any better, but was he keeping up a pretence?

'Do we go on?' I could tell Matt wanted to get this over with.

I raised my hand to stop him. 'Last time David sent me to a grave, said it was my mum.' I looked back up the hill. 'Obviously it wasn't her – but whose grave was it?'

'Couldn't it just have been one of the cavemen?' Matt asked.

'I don't think they do burials.' I put my hand on his shoulder. 'I think we should check it out before we rush in on David.'

I suppose Matt was used to being told what to do, as he'd done in the army, so he shrugged and we went back up and followed the route I had taken before. David had sent me with the chief of the tribe, we'd called him Crow. It wasn't difficult to follow the track, but I did worry again what might have been keeping the tracks well worn. I knew there were sabre tooth tigers near here.

It wasn't long before the path became narrower, closed in by rocks.

'Up there,' I said.

And we found the mound, the one that David had made out to hold my dead mother. The grave hadn't kept all its secrets. I could imagine scavenging animals sniffing in the soil. Or had David left something else buried here?

'Bones,' Matt said and shuddered.

White, bleached bones stuck out from the soil.

'Seen enough?' Matt backed away.

'Hang on.' I knelt down and moved away some of the stones that had been used to make the grave, a skull became partly exposed. I heard a groan from Matt. But I had seen something else. I scrabbled around. This wasn't a caveman grave, I found a watch. It was a watch I recognised. Picking it up there was an inscription on the back. I choked.

"To Tom, from Alvin."

This wasn't my mother's grave. That was my brother's watch. I had given it to him one birthday. This was the brother I thought was in prison with Dad. How had he escaped? What had happened? Was he in this grave?

Matt might not be happy about the grave and the bones, but he must have seen a lot of dead bodies in the trenches. He had joined me on the ground.

'Look.' Matt held up the skull.

The back of the skull had been smashed in.

'Animals?' I said.

I suppose we'd both seen enough police stuff on the TV. This didn't look like damage from animals. It looked as though it had been done with a weapon. I had no idea how my brother could have ended up here. Even though there was no other evidence to prove it was his grave, I was thinking about murder and who had done it.

'David,' I said.

'You can't …' I stopped Matt.

Matt would have told me that a broken skull could mean lots of things, that it was probably the cavemen that had killed him anyway. He would have been right but I wanted to blame David. He was another Tregarthur. It seemed pretty likely to me that if anyone was murdering people it would have been one of that family.

I did my best to cover the grave properly with larger stones and one to mark the spot. I didn't scratch his name. It was still possible this wasn't him, still possible that someone else had taken his watch, I kept it with me.

Before leaving, we checked the cave next to the grave. Before we had found the notebook written by a younger Miss Tregarthur, but now the cave was empty. Everything had been removed. Strange that the watch hadn't been found then.

We made our way back. This time we didn't go quietly. I wanted to let David know that we were coming. As we reached David's hut the two women let out a grunted wail and ran off further down the river. We didn't see them again.

'You.' David struggled to his feet.

I pushed him down again. David wasn't strong and he obviously hadn't fully recovered from the caveman attack. I'd seen him clubbed to the ground. I had thought he was going to be killed. He must have escaped when the cavemen came chasing after us. When they chased us up a tree and were about to stone us to death until the sabre tooth tigers appeared.

'You're going to come with us.' I wasn't going to help him up.

'Why?' he asked.

'We're going home,' I said.

I could see the glint in his eyes. He wouldn't have been strong enough to get back to the tunnel on his own. He must have thought he was stuck here. We were his salvation.

'My sister has come for me?' he sounded more confident. 'That's it. I knew she wouldn't leave me here.'

I shook my head at Matt, seeing he was about to launch into an explanation. We both knew that Miss Tregarthur would have been quite happy to leave people scattered all over time. Even though she had made her promise I wasn't convinced she would have come back for him in the end. I was going to try and do it for her. To bring him back with us. We needed him to come with us. I wasn't going to say anything else, not even accuse him of murder at this moment.

'Your sister will get us home,' I said. I could see he knew there was more, but he wasn't going to hear any more from me.

We had to stay another night. This time around the fire with David. He had managed to survive here by playing at witchdoctor.

'The heads on stakes keep the savages away. But if I need help then I turn the heads around, facing away from the path, then the cavemen aren't so scared.' David wanted to tell us how clever he had been, the small inventions he had made.

'Like the toilet?' he pointed out how he'd managed to channel the water to give him something that didn't stink. 'I got the cavemen to do that in exchange for mending one of their broken legs. They think it's magic.'

I stopped listening. I could see he was just going on because he worried what I might ask. I might have stopped listening but I made sure that Matt or I kept watch through the night.

The only reason he might not kill us was that we were going to take him back to the time tunnel. Perhaps he might have persuaded some of the cavemen to carry him there. Maybe he still worried that he didn't know what he was going to find when we returned.

At least David had more for us to eat. I had forgotten how disgusting mammoth was.

The next day we set off and it was a slow journey, two days of partly carrying David, and he complained all the time. On the way, we heard far off howls, either of men or animals, we saw some mammoths wandering over the grassland. David kept stopping us, saying we should hide. Since we were only hearing noises I made sure we kept going. We finally made it back.

'Where is she?' David shouted as I dumped him on the ground and he saw the rest of our group, but no Alice Tregarthur.

'Wait,' I said. 'Matt, stay with him while I talk this over with Jenna.'

I moved away. David was still calling for his sister.

'Stay there,' I said, as David tried to follow me. 'I need ...' I didn't finish.

First, I left them and ran to the mound of fallen rocks, scrambling up to the Hanging Stones. The air seemed to get colder, mist forming around me.

'Mum,' I called at the stones, feeling stupid – was I really talking to a pile of rocks, or to this strange Hanging Stone? What did I expect? I was stupid. There was no reply in words, but a cold misery seemed to seep out from the ground, traces of mist swirled out, and in my head the echoes of what had been said before, 'Take them all back.'

I shivered and called again and again, there was nothing

more. I went back to the others.

'What are you going to do?' Jenna asked after I had explained about the grave and the watch.

'He must have killed my brother.' I'd taken to hurling stones into the jungle of trees. 'I don't suppose he'll admit it, he's good at telling lies.'

Jenna grabbed my arm as I was about to let loose another stone. She must have seen my anger building up, stones flying further and further. 'Take him to the tunnel.' Jenna pointed at the Hanging Stones. 'Your mum will have to decide what to do.'

'Don't you remember,' I snapped. 'Mum was the one that set out with David, leaving my dad. She may have fallen out with him, but she came here with David. Mum may have taken over the time travel, but she died, I'm not going to get a list of instructions from that pile of rocks.' I pulled away, picking up another stone.

'But …' Jenna started.

'And my brother. How did he get here? They said he was going to jail with Dad, more lies. It seems Mum was telling lies as well.'

'Can you stop chucking things around?' Jack had moved behind me. 'That last one nearly hit Stevie, we're all getting more than worried about you.'

'They think you're turning back into the old Alvin,' Jenna half laughed. 'They aren't worried for you, they're getting scared.'

'Can't we just do what your mum said before she died? Take everyone back,' Jack said. I scowled at him, I was near to attacking anyone.

Jenna saw that, 'No Alvin. Nothing's going to make this go away. You're just going to have to challenge David.'

I stamped back to where Matt was still standing over David. He'd taken to leaning against a rock, trying to look very relaxed and comfortable. I suppose he'd heard most of what I said to the others. My blood was boiling and I had difficulty in keeping my voice quiet, much of my explanation must have been shouted.

I pulled out my brother's watch and threw it at him, catching him on the nose. He gave out a yelp, while I shouted again, 'Explain that.'

David made out he had been hurt badly, calling out for help, 'Keep that maniac away from me.'

No one moved. We waited.

'I've no idea,' David's voice snuffled out as he held his nose.

'You killed my brother.' I couldn't stop. Couldn't wait for his explanation.

'Me? I've never killed anyone,' David sounded so hurt.

He wasn't going to tell me anything. He said he didn't know it was my brother, just someone else who came with Mum, didn't know what had happened to him, 'Just disappeared one day.' There were just too many things that David didn't seem to know, wasn't going to tell.

I was about to jump on him, smash his face with another rock, make him talk. Then Jenna shouted, 'NO.' She had a history of stopping my violent outbursts.

'We just have to take him to the stones and send him back.' Jenna had moved between us. 'Killing him won't make any difference. Come on, let's get rid of him.'

I didn't want to do that. I wanted revenge. 'We don't have to take him back if I kill him,' I snapped. But Jenna had taken hold of me, she was the only one who could have stopped me, but she would always be able to do that.

'Your girlfriend's right, send me back, into the tunnel – if that's what you call it,' David sneered. It wasn't a good idea.

'Shut it,' Jenna snapped at him. Jenna might have stopped me once, but David was doing his best to get me wound up again.

'Let's get him up there.' Jenna pointed to the Hanging Stones on the mound of rubble.

'Good idea.' David got up with a lot less trouble than he'd had before. David seemed a lot more mobile, and cheerful in a very annoying way.

He stumbled up to the Hanging Stones. We followed behind. I was just hoping something bad would happen to him.

David turned, 'Where's the crystal thing?'

I just loved the confusion on his face.

David must have thought that the time travel was still controlled in the only way he knew, by Miss Tregarthur striking her crystal, striking it bringing screaming pain out from the Hanging Stones. The pain that allowed Miss Tregarthur to govern her movement in time. But that had all changed.

'No crystal,' I said with a slight smile.

'Then what? How?' David stammered, his confidence lost.

'You'll find out,' I said and pushed him forward.

Something stirred around the stones, almost like steam appearing, different colours, before a blue mist curled up in a spiral. Blue mist had seemed to be a good signal, one that had sent people back to their homes.

'See you all,' David gave us a big grin. 'Or maybe I won't, ha ha.'

The mist changed. A new colour, blood red. David lost his grin, tried to turn back and couldn't.

'Theresa, NO,' screamed David, using my mum's name. He was being drawn into the mist, pulled towards a gap opening below the Hanging Stones. 'NO, it wasn't like that.'

Perhaps he understood. There was no Jenna to stop what was happening in this time tunnel. Maybe it was taking him home – a very long route. Maybe he wasn't going to go anywhere. He was another person I never saw or heard of again. David's screaming disappeared with him. One down. We had more people to find, people left in the wrong time.

13

A MAN OF WAR

We were still standing on the mound in front of the Hanging Stones. The mist had cleared. David had gone. I looked at the others: Jack and Mary stood close together, with Matt and Stevie slightly further away. Stevie had started jerking his head to one side, over and over. Matt told him to stop, but it just slowed him for a while. Jack said it was all because of the war.

'You need to tell them,' Jenna said, and gave me another hug.

I could see that all of them needed to be talked to – but by someone who knew what to say, and I didn't believe that was something I could do. Well it wasn't, until Jenna stopped hugging and started poking me.

'Right,' I said, searching for better words. 'If we are going to get other people out of the wrong time, we have to move on, and …' I realised what needed to be said and I didn't know a good way of starting.

'On to the Black Death?' Jack found the words.

I could see we had to move to the next time we had been sent to, and that was the time of the plague, the disease that caused so many deaths across the world. Mary and Jack explained all the details of the disease to Matt and Stevie. They were the two experts. The explanation didn't make Stevie's jerking any better.

Jenna drew me to one side while they talked.

'Do we all have to go?' Jenna said.

'No idea,' I replied. 'I suppose it depends what happens in the time tunnel.'

'But that's your mum, she's in control now,' Jenna pleaded. 'We don't want to take them all with us, one of them is sure to catch the plague. We don't want more deaths. Can't you see if you can get the tunnel to take the others home?'

'We are coming, whatever you say,' Mary had obviously overheard Jenna's words.

I could see that bothered Jenna, and she was trying not to say anything – yet.

Matt and Stevie seemed to separate themselves. They weren't demanding to come with us. I knew they needed to go home. I could see that Matt would have been useful if it came to a fight, but I thought the two of them had had enough of fighting. With no further discussion, I led them back up to the Hanging Stones.

'Do you talk to it? I mean her,' Matt quickly corrected himself.

'Not exactly,' I answered, because I had no idea what would happen. But it seemed that the tunnel took the decision. As we neared the stones, a blue mist rose from the ground.

'It'll be ok,' I said and pushed the two of them forward and within seconds they disappeared. I just had to hope they would be safe, and I went back to the other three who were starting to argue.

'If we all go back to the time of the Black Death,' Jenna hadn't been able to keep quiet. 'Then one of us is bound to catch it, better if Alvin and I go alone.'

'That isn't going to happen,' Mary sounded firm. 'We said we would go back for Kan. We made that promise.'

I heard her say that as I joined them, remembering it was actually me who had promised Kan that we would return. Even when I said it, I didn't think it would be a promise I could keep.

That wasn't going to be the only problem. Kan hadn't followed us into the time tunnel before, he had decided to stay behind with the love of his life - Posy. He'd ridden a horse away with them both escaping from everything. Why would he come with us if we went back to him again?

Kan and Van, the two brothers who had been pitched into the time of King Edward and the Black Death. Their easy craziness fitted with the jousting, hunting, and fighting. Until Van was killed. But getting Kan back was only part of what we faced.

The other problem might be even more difficult – last time we had escaped we only just avoided the crowd of villagers who were going to burn us to death for blasphemy. A crowd led by a priest screaming for them to kill us. If we went back, we might just meet up with the same lot, ready with their fire. Even if we avoided them we would be right into the village where so many had died from the plague. Jenna was right, we were pretty certain to catch it. I didn't think it mattered how many we took with us.

My opinion didn't seem to count in this argument. By the time I'd finished thinking how hard it was going to be, the others had agreed we would all go together. Part of me thought I should try to get Mum to let me do it on my own, but even I could see I would need help.

'Can't go now,' Jack said. 'It's getting late.'

'Would it be the same if we went to a different time?' Mary asked Jack. He had become the time travel expert.

'Probably,' Jack said.

I had no idea where he found the certainty in his voice.

'In that case we need a fire,' Jenna said, looking at Jack, who even in the mess we were in still managed to laugh. Jack had become a bit of an expert with fires as well as time.

Jack had us search for some dry moss and twigs. Then, hitting two pieces of flint together, he soon made enough sparks to start it off and with a lot of blowing he had a fire. We were impressed.

That night Jenna made a chuckern stew. She'd rescued one of the cooking pots. That was the thing she picked up as we ran out of the cave as the rocks swallowed up my mother. I didn't have any idea how she'd managed to do that in the middle of such chaos. And not break it.

'Great job,' I said, but I was not really too enthusiastic for the stew which had kept us alive. Jenna scowled at me.

It wasn't just the taste that troubled me. The stew of those strange birds – half chicken, half duck. They'd kept us alive but had killed Susie because at first we hadn't cleaned them properly or cooked them well. I remembered her dying, I remembered carrying her to the gravesite.

'When we do go, we need to get in and out in a hurry,' I said wanting to move the conversation away from the stew. 'The quicker we do it then it has to make it less dangerous – this Black Death thing.'

'That's not going to be easy. We don't know if Kan will have returned to the village. They were going to burn him as well.' Jack was looking at Mary. Was it just Mary who wanted to go back?

'We have to hope we get there when the mob has quietened down,' Jenna said.

'Quiet or all dead,' I added. I could see that didn't go down well so I went on: 'It's the only thing we can do – go back to the village and see what happens.'

So, the next day we did.

The Hanging Stones were surrounded by mist, difficult to say whether there was a colour or not, mostly haze, maybe green. I could feel something as we came up to them, but this wasn't like the anger we had felt in the time tunnel before. I tried to call out but while I could feel a sort of vibration, there were no words. Whatever had happened to my mum, it wasn't the same as Miss Tregarthur. Maybe it took time to work it out – that just felt weird, time to sort out being swallowed into the rocks and controlling time?

'Come on,' I said, leading them into the mist. I could tell they all felt that I was in charge here. It wasn't what I felt.

This time there was no whirling, tumbling feeling. It happened slowly. The mist shimmered, the ground trembled. The mist grew dark, thick, and choking before it cleared as though it had been sucked away.

As it cleared we saw the moor stretched out, dark wet and bleak as always, but such a view. We stood for a while, just watching the clouds skit across the sky, some low enough to touch the dark pillars of rock standing on top of the tors. This wasn't a pre-historic landscape anymore, we were back into something more usual, well maybe only a few hundred years unusual.

'Sheep,' Jack said as though the white dots scattered over the moor were a surprise. And I suppose they were, sheep at least meant we were not in the time of sabre tooth tigers and mammoths. There was nothing else to tell us what year we had arrived back here. No aeroplanes, no noise of modern life, no cars in the distance, just the moor and the few sheep.

'At least there isn't anyone ready to carry out that death sentence.' Jenna was still looking around nervously. I nodded.

None of us would forget that crowd of villagers, screaming as they chased us, saying we were witches and had to be burnt. That was all part of Miss Tregarthur's revenge, wanting to punish me for stopping her terrible plans, even if a death sentence might seem more than a little harsh.

'Down to the village?' Mary asked.

We all knew that was where we needed to go, and if this was the time of the plague, it was a village of danger. Last time Mary had brought a cure, some of her brother's antibiotics, pills used for acne in our time which had saved a life in another age – the life of a king. Mary had none of them left. But we did know that travelling to a different time seemed to be its own cure. I guess if you travel to a time when you didn't have the disease or whatever, then it seemed to disappear. Or something else which wasn't understandable.

'Demelza and Zach got over the plague.' Jenna seemed to have been reading my thoughts, again. She was good at that. 'They didn't have this black death when we met them again.'

'That was a pity,' I said under my breath.

'Will that work for us?' Jack muttered as we set off.

We walked down a muddy track. A track probably made by sheep and whoever looked after them, maybe some other people walking over the moor, if that was what people did – go walking. Probably they spent most of their time trying to stay alive rather than going out for a hike. I didn't think people had many holidays in the time of the Black Death.

I suppose we had all been wrapped up in our own thoughts, plodding on with no talking until we reached the stream in the valley.

'The hut,' I shouted, seeing a broken-down small building near to the stream. Not much of it was left, the walls had fallen in. A sheep was ripping at tufts of grass growing out of the remains of the fireplace. The hut had been a place for a shepherd to shelter. There was no shelter now.

'No body,' I said. Last time we had found the shepherd, dead from the Black Death.

'It must mean we have come back to a later time.' Jack was looking around the fallen building. 'The hut was still standing last time.'

Once we'd thought that the time tunnel had limits. It wouldn't move you back to a time earlier than you had travelled before. I think we were wrong. Anyway it probably changed when a new person was taken into the stones. That made me think of Mum again, I'd almost got used to her being dead before we went back and carried her into the tunnel. But wasn't she going to live forever, she would be a part of the moor? Until …

'Move on,' I said not wanting to go over the thought of why my mother might not be in a forever place, why someone else might take over – when they died. I shivered, even though it wasn't cold – just damp – out here.

We pushed on, up the small hill, and through the wood. More of a track. A dog barked in the distance, we started to smell wood smoke. Once there had been a gate across this path, it hung broken and rotten at the side. Ahead we could see a few houses, a man came out of one. He shuffled out, head down, as though the world was on his shoulders. I think he might have seen us but looked away and shuffled faster down the track.

'Lucky,' Jenna said.

'I don't think it was luck.' Mary moved to the front with her hands out, stopping us. 'If this is the Black Death, then we've no idea what his life is like, how many deaths he's seen. He won't want to have anything to do with strangers.'

'He might tell other people.' Jack looked around but no one else was about.

'Might not be anyone to tell.' I thought that was more like the truth.

'But we are strange,' Jenna said. 'We've got to keep out of sight. Look at us.'

We were in much more modern gear. Mary was the only one in farm clothes that might have blended in, the rest of us were in army gear. Jenna still had medals. Mary was right, we needed to keep hidden, but that was impossible. There was only one track through the village, past the church.

'We should wait until it gets dark,' Jack said and we stopped.

'Back into the wood.' Jenna turned and we went back.

We stopped in the trees at the edge of the moor, next to a small stream. Looking out on the moor, it was a bleak and wild place. We could just see one of the peaks in the distance. As darkness started to fall it didn't feel a friendly place. It didn't make me feel hopeful about finding Kan or getting anyone back to the right time, it was too big a task. I guess we all felt like that, sitting in the evening silence.

Jenna jumped up, 'More chuckern,' she said, trying to be cheerful. 'I saved some.'

'Picnic,' Mary joined her.

That might have made things better but I kept thinking it had been a long time since we had felt safe enough to enjoy a picnic, a very long time, thousands of years.

Full darkness never came, this had to be summer. Some light remained in the sky. But the night brought a chill in the air, a breeze was starting up, coming straight off the tors. A thin moon rose over the hills.

'Watch for dogs,' Jenna said as we walked back into the village.

'We'll have to ask in the pub,' I said.

There was no pub. Had there been a pub, an inn, in the time of the Black Death? I couldn't remember.

'We have to go through the village.' Jenna walked on.

Go through the village and hope, I thought.

14

NOT THE EASY WAY

Despite our worries, it was not hard to find the place where Kan lived. On the other edge of the village was a small house, mostly wood, not in great shape, but still standing, which wasn't the case for many of the buildings we passed.

But the state of the building wasn't what gave away that this could be the place Kan lived. Outside was the largest horse I had ever seen, a beast that could only be used for war, its eyes seemed to blaze at us, catching the faint moonlight. It pawed at the ground, huge hooves with metal guards, metal armour plates shielding its legs, over its back a blanket with an emblem we had seen before, the emblem of the king. The horse looked away and carried on grazing.

'Has to be Kan,' I said. 'If he's alive then this has to be him, no one else in this village was up to fighting in a real war. No one else would have a horse like this.'

Without asking the others I walked up to the front door. It stood slightly open, inside I could hear noises. One voice. One voice sounding as though the world had ended, crying: 'No, No,' over and over. I walked in. A single candle gave a dim light in the bare room.

It was Kan and I startled him. Suddenly I had a sword at my neck. I had hardly seen him move, a blur from a man who knew what to do when disturbed.

'It's me,' I gasped, probably the most stupid thing to say but it was all I could think of. Kan dropped the sword and it clattered on the floor. He turned back to the bed where he had been sitting. Posy lay there.

Kan saw Mary and jumped up again, grabbing her by the neck of her tunic, 'Quick, give me those pills.'

Mary shook her head. She had no pills, no antibiotic cure this time. Kan fell back on the bed, holding Posy's hand. Her pale face was marked with dark blotches, she coughed and a trickle of blood escaped from her lips, she gave out a weak groan. She tried to move but her thin body had no strength.

'Easy, love.' Kan wiped her forehead.

The Black Death was here. Posy was near to her end, Kan was destroyed.

'I'm only back a few days,' Kan's voice cracked. 'Back from France.' He looked up at us, red-eyed, his face creased with exhaustion. 'It's the war, you know.' He turned away again, back to Posy.

I heard a mutter from Mary about this being the Hundred Years war. She had said something about that when we'd been here before. The sort of thing that didn't make sense to people who had only just started fighting and her words didn't make this feel any better now. We were never far away from wars.

'It was the only way to make money,' Kan started again. I didn't believe him. After his brother had died, murdered by the king's men, Kan was a man who was going to war, even if he'd had to start it himself.

Slowly he gave us more of the story, how he'd left Posy behind and set off to join the army. He'd just returned, along with his warhorse, not knowing that Posy had caught the plague.

'There's not many left in this village, most dead or left, just a few hanging on, too old or sick to get out,' Kan's voice grew stronger. 'At least there aren't any priests or burning parties,' Kan spat his words. He was still an angry man. He still didn't leave Posy's side.

Mary searched around and found a jug of weak beer, it was what they drank, and a stale loaf of bread. She tried to give some to Kan but he shrugged her off. Whatever spark had driven him was fast going out.

'Kan,' Jenna stood over him speaking softly. 'We need to take you home.'

I could see that Jenna was going to explain why we needed him to come with us, but I could also see that it meant nothing to Kan. Posy had been the reason he'd stayed in this time, and I couldn't see that he would ever leave her. Even if Posy survived being taken back to the Hanging Stones, we had never been able to take anyone from their own time. Miss Tregarthur had managed to create her awful loop bringing the cave people, but we had no idea how she managed to do it. Would Mum be able to make something like that work?

Jenna pushed the four of us back out of the house, leaving Kan who didn't seem to care what we did. He certainly hadn't responded when Jenna suggested we take him.

Outside we stood in silence for a moment.

'He won't come,' Jenna said what we all knew.

'Do we try to take Posy back with us?' I said.

'I don't think she would survive, even if we carried her to

the Hanging Stones,' Mary paused, but went on. 'She's so near to death.'

'Do we wait and try later?' I wondered if we had to wait here until Posy died and then we'd try and persuade Kan to come.

'We can't,' Mary's voice was more of a plea. 'We'll all get this disease. Have you …' she stopped. Standing in the cool dark with the palest of moons, I just knew what she was going to say. 'Did you notice those marks on his neck?'

I had and tried not to think of it. I didn't know how long Kan had actually been back from France, whether that mattered anyway, but Kan had caught the plague. The marks that stood out on his neck were the sign of the Black Death.

At that moment Kan slipped into the middle of our group. 'I'm not coming, I will die here with her, I have nothing else, you will not take me away.'

Looking at Kan, we'd have needed an army. Fighting had made him huge and strong, with the confidence to mean what he said. He wasn't going to come with us. Whatever my mum had said about taking everyone back, we were not taking Kan. We said nothing as he returned to Posy's bedside.

'Kan, wait,' cried Jenna.

'I will not come.' Kan disappeared back into the house.

I stepped forward, maybe I should try. I felt Jack grab my shoulder, holding me back. I turned to him, he shook his head.

Jack whispered, 'He won't come unless we take Posy and we can't take her whatever happens.'

'Why?' This sounded complicated.

'If she did manage to come with us, we would be taking her out of her own time,' Jack said. Even in almost darkness I think Jack must have seen confusion on my face.

Jack went on: 'It would be just the same as leaving people behind, people in the wrong time. Your mother said it would never stop until we got everyone home. It is the only chance we have to stop Miss Tregarthur's loop of the First World War, otherwise it will never end, the future that we know will never happen. We can't take Posy because she would just become another time problem.'

I wanted something else to be the truth. 'We don't know …' I said, but Jack's words sounded like the awful truth, and there was one more thing that I wasn't going to say.

Mary said it for me, 'We don't have to take dead people back.'

We could leave Kan here with Posy, he had caught the plague. He would soon be dead like the others who caught this terrible disease. His death would mean our job was done in this time.

'Well, I'm going to try again.' Jenna went for the door.

Kan stood before her, holding his sword, 'No you won't, you will leave, forget me, go home, just say a few words in the graveyard before you go.' With that he slammed the door.

'It's only me, my love.' His door slamming must have disturbed Posy. Kan's words were never those of a school kid, he wasn't a teenager, he had grown to be a man. His war hadn't been the life of terror that Stevie and Matt had faced, Kan's war had been something different and Kan had always been different. He and his brother – Van – had brought their strength to save us when we had been sent to this time. We had to leave him, but only after we had visited the grave of his brother. Kan was right, he would die in this age of the Black Death, he had nowhere else to go, no one else to go to.

That had been the reason they had come to help us. Jack had brought them through the time tunnel, Kan and his brother

Van, not even their real names. They had been escaping their own troubles at home. There was nothing for them to go back to, no reason to return.

We walked away in silence, up to the church, into the graveyard to find the huge stone that we had used to mark his brother's grave. The grave of Van, another death, Van who had been murdered by the king's men, confused with his twin brother Kan. It wouldn't have mattered which of them had died first, to be separated had destroyed them. They had followed us into time, for them it had seemed like a joke, a bit of danger perhaps, but they had not been expecting it to be so dangerous as to kill them both.

Miss Tregarthur's world wasn't a place where teenagers had fun in any of the usual sorts of ways. Miss Tregarthur's fun was death.

We had stood over other graves and we had never found the right words to say. I tried to say goodbye but the words wouldn't come. I felt tears on my face, as we left. Miss Tregarthur might be finished but her terrible legacy was not over.

We planned to spend the night in the wood again before setting off for the Hanging Stones. Again, it was a silent journey into the wood. I was going over and over what had happened on this last night. I did not feel good about it. Had we left Kan for his sake or for ours? Leaving him to die an awful death meant we had left no one alive and out of time in the world of the Black Death. We had done nothing for them.

'We should have stayed,' I said. I wanted to stop, go back and take the others with me, but I kept walking.

'SHOULDN'T WE?' I shouted to the moor.

Jenna put her arms around me, hugged me tight. I felt Jack and Mary close in on us. A group hug in the middle of the bleak moor, a place that stood its own place in time. We walked on.

'If Posy died, if we'd waited then we could have taken Kan. He would have recovered if we'd taken him home, recovered in the tunnel.' My voice was a moan, each step was a moan.

'He wouldn't have come,' Jenna answered. 'He would have stayed, there was nothing for him at home, he said that when he came to help us. Nothing but trouble, he would not have come.'

'Shouldn't we have tried harder?' I said.

'No.' Mary made us all stop. 'Look, what would we have waited for? Posy looked near to death, but we've seen it doesn't always work like that, she might survive for several more days, but death might just come to Kan before that, then what would we do?'

I sort of felt that was right, but part of me still felt we were making up a story, a reason to justify what we had done. We walked on. It was no good.

I would like to think it was me, probably it was Jenna, but we just seemed to turn. With no talking, we were all headed back to the village.

We came around to their house from the other side. We did see one more person even at this time in the night but they hurried away, definitely no one wanted to meet strangers in the dark. They might have wanted to burn us before but death had torn this place apart.

We reached the Kans' door, closed. Jenna pushed forward. I pulled her back. We could hear no sound from inside.

'Wait.' I knocked on the wood. There was no reply. I knocked again. I pushed and the door swung wide.

I knew as I stepped inside that it would be bad, I think I knew even when we turned back from the moor.

They lay together on the bed. Posy could have been asleep, peaceful if it wasn't for the blood seeping through her tunic. Kan had his sword buried deep in his own chest. Had he fallen on it and found enough strength to stagger to the bed? Did he look at peace? I wanted to believe he was finally at peace, but he didn't look like that. His face was twisted. This had not been the easy way.

We left them. Should we have buried them? We were not that good. I wanted to run as fast and as far as I could. I could not bear to see those dead faces again, none of us could. So many deaths, would it ever stop? What happened in that house would never leave me. We owed Kan and his brother so much, we were leaving them dead with no one to remember them in this time.

We left. We had to make for the Hanging Stones. Stumbling in the dark we went on. In the end, we had to stop. We couldn't find any path and kept falling over rocks and into bog. We sat in a circle, silent again, and waiting for light before setting off again.

In the early light, we reached the hill, sheltering beneath an overhang near to the stream. The weather was as gloomy as we were, drizzle was becoming more like rain.

'We're not doing well,' Jenna said. 'Not getting any good people back home, we've only sent that awful David home. I would have swapped him for Kan anytime.' Jenna pulled me closer and said quietly, 'You know we need to work out what we are going to do before we get to the next time.'

I nodded.

'Where are we going?' Jack asked.

We hadn't worked anything out, it was too difficult. Jenna and I looked at each other. There were more problems in the next time place on the list, more problems than just getting the people we had left. Last time Ivy and Sam had found themselves trapped with us. It had just been the four of us, well mostly four. Four and a bit.

'I think it's time for you to go home,' I said, thinking that would be easier than explaining what we had to do.

'No chance,' Jack and Mary said together.

But these two weren't like Kan. I could see they weren't going to argue that much. And by the time we had climbed back up the hill to the Hanging Stones, they weren't really protesting. We hugged and said we'd meet at home, hugged and lied. We had no idea where or when we might meet, but Jack and Mary went into the tunnel's mist, into a blue haze which had seemed to mean home before. Of course, we didn't know what home would be, if we couldn't correct things then they might end up back in that war. Difficult to feel that war might be going on at the same time as we were standing on the top of this hill, hundreds of years before it had started.

Jenna and I saw them disappear before the mist changed. This time the moorland air hung loose and cold, cutting through me. No words, but it felt as if something bad, something very bad was coming. Not coming here, but coming to the next place we had to travel.

We stepped forward, as the mist gathered again and we moved

in the air, I could feel the terrible sadness in the journey, the terrible sadness of my mum. Whatever we were going to find would be harder than we had imagined, and we had already imagined that it would be worse than hard.

15

MEASLES

It felt as though we hadn't moved. Once again, the moor stretched out in front of us, the dark stones, the mist, the high tors against the skyline. Again, no noise of modern life. Not much rain.

'What are we going to do about the baby?' Jenna asked the obvious question but there were others that still worried me. However, I had absolutely no answer to what we would do about the baby.

The time we hoped we had arrived at, that's if the tunnel had brought us back, was sometime in the 1830s. Before, it had been Miss Tregarthur again. Jenna and Ivy had been sentenced to be transported to Australia. Sam and I had been sentenced to hang.

Ivy was a very different person to Jenna, much less able to deal with the terrible journey on the boats. Ivy had been picked out by one of the crew, the result was a baby.

I had never asked what happened on the boats, never asked Jenna, but I know she had suffered such a hard time. Often there was a look in her eyes that told me she was thinking of that time.

Sam and I, escaping from the hangman had worked our way across the world, finally meeting up with Ivy and Jenna in South West Australia.

'Did you think that Sam would feel that way about the baby? It wasn't his,' I asked Jen. Sam had, pretty immediately, taken on helping Ivy with her baby.

'He was in love with Ivy, didn't matter what had happened to her,' Jenna said while staring at the ground. 'That's why they called the baby Sam as well, baby Sam.'

'I suppose it made a difference that the crew man, the father, died,' I said, more wanting something to say and I knew it sounded stupid. Of course it made a difference. If the man hadn't died he was going to keep Ivy as a near slave. They would never have escaped easily.

Jenna didn't seem to pick up on my anxiety, or maybe she knew she just needed to move away from talking about life on the transport ships.

'Ivy isn't going to leave the baby here – might be quite a lot older by now,' Jenna was still looking at the ground. 'Do you …'

'No,' I said, no I didn't want to hear what had happened to Jenna. 'But I think we are going to get some help with your question.' I pointed across the top of the hill. Sam and Ivy were coming towards us, just Sam and Ivy.

They arrived in silence. Ivy and Jenna hugged, Sam and I nodded at each other. This was a traditional male and female meeting up. I didn't hug Sam because I was waiting to hear the worst. I think that was the reason.

'Measles,' Sam said quietly, before both he and Ivy crashed into each other, clinging and sobbing.

Jenna and I stood and waited.

'Did …' I started.

'Wait,' Jenna hissed and gave me one of her pokes.

It took a while. Through the sobs, we got the story of how baby Sam had caught measles.

'It was the people arriving at the town. They'd come from England. They brought measles with them,' Ivy said.

Obviously, there were no vaccinations, the baby was sick for weeks, becoming weaker and weaker.

'There was nothing we could do.' Ivy wiped away her tears. 'No treatment, no hospital, no anything. Sam wasn't the only baby to die.'

Now, I knew I wasn't the most wonderful person in the world, or the most caring and that was why Jenna watched me very closely. Still, I liked to think that I didn't breathe any sighs of relief. Surely, nothing could be further from my mind than finding the problem of baby Sam had just disappeared? But I can't say that was the absolute truth.

We just had no idea whether baby Sam would have been able to travel in the time tunnel. Only people from different ages seemed to travel with us. Baby Sam, being half Ivy might have been able to come. Or would it cause the same problem Jack had talked about. If Posy had come with us would we have started off another issue in time?

But that's not what I was thinking, it was worse. Suppose the time tunnel had ripped the baby in half, half with us, half staying behind. I know that was a crazy awful thought but the other thought was seeing Ivy refusing to come with us, refusing and that might stop us having any chance of stopping this terrible mess left by Miss Tregarthur.

So, Jenna might have been forgiven for watching to see any signs of my sigh of relief. With the baby dead, we could return. Well, almost.

'How did you get back from Australia?' I asked moving on to a safer subject, I hoped.

'After the baby died ...' Ivy started but couldn't go on.

'I found a job on a ship as a cook,' Sam explained. 'They gave us a cabin instead of payment.'

'What happened when you got back? Didn't you get arrested?' I said. We had all been found guilty in a rigged court. Jenna and I had nearly been recaptured when we had returned from Australia.

'The captain got all our papers sorted out,' Ivy found the strength to go on. 'Lots of convicts were coming back to England. They didn't really want convicted criminals in that part of Australia. They made them free men and women. So, there was no problem.'

'But why ...' I started.

Sam interrupted, 'Why didn't we stay? We didn't stay because every minute there reminded us of the baby, neither of us could deal with that.' Ivy held on to Sam. A thought just flashed through my head – that could have been me. It could have happened to Jenna. Would I have been as good and supportive as Sam? I caught the look from Jenna. Lucky I didn't have to find out.

'But why have you come here, come back to the moor? How did you know we would be here?' I asked.

'We came back to England months ago, I got another job with a butcher, Ivy is helping in a school,' Sam said. 'We decided that we would come back to the moor once a week. It was our only chance, we felt you might come back.'

'The only thing we had to hold on to was your mother's words,' Ivy said.

I looked puzzled, how did they know what Mum had said?

'We were there.' Sam saw the look on my face. 'In the battle between the cavemen. Don't you remember? Ivy broke her arm?'

'Right,' I said, but it was hard to remember.

'It's better now,' Ivy said, lifting her arm. 'Seemed to mend itself when we moved to a different time.'

'That was when your mother told you that nothing would stop unless you got everyone back home,' Sam sounded frustrated that we didn't see the importance of this.

'We hoped that meant you'd come back for us.' Ivy's stare felt as though this wasn't the whole story.

Maybe Ivy had thought we'd come for her, but maybe she didn't care what happened. The baby's death was still so raw. But coming here each week? It didn't seem likely to work. But was there something I had missed. Was it something to do with the tunnel? Was Mum learning how to control other events, not just time? That certainly seemed to have been something Miss Tregarthur had done.

'So, we can go home?' Sam looked towards the Hanging Stones.

'There's Hugh,' I said.

'Jailbreak Hugh?' Sam looked puzzled.

'Who?' asked Ivy.

Hugh was difficult to explain. He had once saved Sam and me from being hanged by setting up a jailbreak. His help didn't last and later he tried to get us sent back to prison. He was probably related to Alice Tregarthur, maybe a step-brother, but there were a lot of lies that stuck to Hugh. He seemed to be part of Miss Tregarthur's money making plans, something to do with selling gas pipes.

Whatever, he was terrified of his so-called step-sister, she seemed to be holding him captive in this part of history. He wasn't the bravest of people, but despite changing his mind, he had saved my life. And we had to get him back home to his own time. We hadn't had much luck doing that sort of thing so far.

'Maybe he will want to come with us,' Jenna said after we'd been talking about Hugh for a while, talking and walking back down the hill. Sam and Ivy were taking us to the small house they lived in. 'The house came with the teaching job,' Ivy had said.

I thought about Jenna's suggestion. Would Hugh want to come with us? He might just decide to get us sent back to jail. How were we going to find out?

We stayed the night in their little stone house. It reminded me of the house in Australia, a white painted, thatched cottage, similar to other houses around. Ivy had a small garden where she grew her herbs.

'Even if we get everyone back, it's not going make everything better,' I was speaking my thoughts aloud. I was thinking of the baby.

Jenna had been listening, 'I spoke to Jack about that. About what happened when he had returned home the first time?'

I had forgotten. So much had happened. When Sam told me about Mum's words, it hadn't felt completely real. So much mess, so many deaths.

Jenna was watching me. 'Can't you remember?' she said gently.

I wasn't sure if I didn't remember things or didn't want to remember them.

Jenna went on: 'Jack was the one who found the time tunnel again.'

158

'Eh?'

'Back in the caveman time. Jack and you moved all those rocks, re-discovered the tunnel. That's when most of the others left, went home.' Jenna's words brought back more of the memory.

Jack had left the caveman world and returned home with most of the others who had come out on Miss Tregarthur's terrible school hike.

'It seemed to help us,' I said, thinking back. 'The time tunnel wasn't always evil.'

My thoughts became clearer. Before she had taken over, the spirit in the time tunnel had been her sister who Miss Tregarthur had tormented to carry out her plans. But it seemed as though her sister sometimes had the strength to rebel, to help us. It didn't last.

Jack had been home. But Mary and Jack had come back into the mess of time to help us – bringing Kan and Van. Some of the travel had helped, until Miss Tregarthur managed to destroy all that.

'Jack said that he couldn't remember much about the time travel, when he got home he had flashes of remembering but it all seemed hazy,' Jenna said. 'Maybe it will help if Ivy doesn't remember.'

I doubted that would work. I was more worried that Ivy would have terrible flashes of her baby dying. Would Sam stay with her? Would any of us stay together?

We talked through most of the night, talking and trying to make plans and sense of what had happened. But there was still one huge hole in any plans we might make - cavemen. How were we going to get any of them back in their real time?

Very early the next morning Jenna and I set off to look for Hugh. We borrowed clothes from Ivy and Sam. I might have got away with my army uniform, which had become quite grubby, but Jenna's Field Marshall get up really made her stand out.

Ivy and Sam went back to work. They were used to it. I wasn't sure why they carried on as usual. We could probably have sent them home in the time tunnel, but they wanted to stay. I asked Jenna if she knew why.

'I don't know really, but it has to be about the baby. When they go home it will be as though there never was one. If we did get everything back to normal, what will Ivy's normal be? She may be a woman here, with a job and a house and everything, but if she gets back home she'll still be at school. I think she's scared of that.'

'Like we were,' I said, putting my arm around her. Life at home had seemed so terrible that Jenna and I had planned to stay in the caveman world, trying to build a life in that time thousands of years ago. It seemed quite stupid now, and after everything we had been through I wanted to get home. I felt I could sort it out, I had learnt a lot about sorting things out.

'We can't sort it out if the war is still going on,' Jenna, again seemed to read my thoughts.

Sam had fixed us a lift. A cart went down to the city once a week.

'We send down meat and other things,' Sam had said. 'They like my sausages.'

I could see why they weren't exactly in a hurry to leave. They were organised here, in control, not like we all would be if we returned home – it would be back to other people telling us what to do. Not that I had much habit of doing what they said.

The cart bumped us along. Last time we'd been on this road it was as prisoners being taken to the courthouse and we should have ended on the gallows. Thinking about that reminded me that we were probably still wanted criminals. I wasn't going to suggest disguising ourselves – remembering how much fun Jenna would have reminding me about the dress I had to wear last time.

The trip took the whole day, bumping up and down and eating the bread and cheese we'd been given.

'We don't eat much of the meat,' Sam had said giving us the food. 'It's too expensive for poor people like us. We just sell it.'

Nearing the town, we took to walking. The cart driver hadn't talked to us, he seemed lost in his own thoughts, although often shouting to people on the way. He seemed to know all the people we saw. I suppose he passed them every time he went to the town.

He had dropped us at a crossroad, told us when he would return. We could meet him. I wondered if he would take Hugh, maybe Hugh who didn't want to be taken.

Again, the first thing we noticed as we walked was the smell and it got worse as we passed more houses. We were coming down a hill and the town stretched out in front of us with the sea beyond.

'We have to make for the waterside, find that place, what was it called?' I said as we reached another crossroad.

'The Pool.' Jenna looked ahead, but we still had a way to go before we reached the main part of town. We didn't stop – I didn't want to find out if they still wanted to arrest me. Whatever time we were in, I guessed that hanging was still on the list of punishments.

We didn't want to ask anyone for directions. So it took a while as we tried to remember the route. But we followed the shore line and with the smell getting even worse it wasn't hard to find the Pool. A collection of houses stood around a small quay with a couple of boats tied up but sitting on sand at the bottom. It must have been low tide. The stench coming up at us made me retch. The buildings were wooden and looked chaotic, as though they were built by sticking more and more rooms on to whatever had been there before. This was not a rich part of town.

One of the buildings was the Inn we had stayed at before. The inn sign had gone and the windows were boarded up. It was the place where we had helped make illegal gin when we'd been here before. I knew they were going to get caught and the landlord drank most of what we made.

'That way,' Jenna pointed up ahead, with her hand over her nose.

I nodded and we left quickly, taking the road out of town, hoping it led to the house where Hugh had lived before. He'd called himself Mr Connoy. We had no idea whether he still lived there, but asking questions had always brought trouble around here and we didn't want to ask any more.

We saw Hugh's house in the distance, but more houses had been built since we were last here and it wasn't so isolated. Dogs barked as we passed those houses. Hugh had a dog, if he still lived in the same place.

The house looked the same, but had not been well looked after. At the front was a large pile of iron pipes, rusting and covered in weeds. There was no barking.

'Doesn't look like he made much money,' I said pointing

at the pipes.

'At least if the pipes are here, he may be as well,' said Jenna, pulling me to a halt.

We'd had spent ages talking about what we would do when we got here. Talking and not deciding. Eventually we had decided, or Jenna had decided, that she would go in alone.

'You might frighten him,' Jenna had said.

I knew that wasn't her reason, Jenna could be a lot scarier than me. But if Hugh was anything like the man he'd been before then Jenna's idea was a good one. I went round to the back of the house, into the yard where more rusting pipes were piled.

I heard shouting, something crashed and Hugh hurtled out of his back door. I stuck out my leg. Hugh tumbled into the yard, falling into the pipes and howling in pain. Jenna came out after him.

'You didn't frighten him then?' I laughed.

Hugh was still scrabbling to get to his feet, I pushed him down again. I know this was the sort of thing my dad would have been good at, but it still felt weird that I should be pushing people around. But if I hadn't learnt to do that we would have been dead a long time ago – a very long time ago. Jenna and I had done a lot of pushing around. Not sure how that would work if we got home.

'You,' Hugh shouted. 'Why do you keep coming back?'

'I just wanted to ask you about last time,' I looked down at him. 'When you were trying to get us sent back to the court?'

'I … I …,' Hugh blurted and made no sense.

'Don't worry,' Jenna said. 'We've come to take you home.'

I have never seen anyone change so quickly.

Hugh's face sagged, his whole body sagged, 'Home, I want

163

to go home, she won't let me, I can't go, I have to sell these pipes, no one wanted to buy them, they're the wrong size, it's hopeless, she won't let me go.' His voice trailed off, he didn't try to get up, he just fell back into the pipes with a groan.

I pulled him up. 'She is dead and gone. Miss Tregarthur does not exist, not live and walking about or even dead and inside the stones of the moor. She has gone.'

''But she was here, yesterday,' Hugh gasped.

'That's time travel for you, but she won't be coming again,' I said, but I had no idea whether that was true, was Miss Tregarthur actually still roaming around in time? I really didn't want to meet her again.

It took a lot more explaining. Hugh didn't believe us, but he did want to. We were his only hope. I knew we had to get him away immediately, but the day was ending, we would have to stay here overnight. We couldn't trust Hugh, he could easily change his mind, he could still get us sent back to jail.

'The barn,' Jenna suggested.

Hugh had tricked us into a barn where he was storing the iron pipes last time. Tricked us and locked us in. This time Hugh didn't go in without a struggle, but it was worth it. We left him there while we searched his house and ate his food.

'These could come in handy,' I had found a purse hidden amongst a pile of Hugh's clothes. A good hiding place, the clothes stank, but it was a purse. Only three gold coins, it could have held a lot more. They had to have belonged to Miss Tregarthur. Gold was ideal for travelling in time, valuable in any part of history where money was used.

We took Hugh a lump of bread and a bottle of beer from his kitchen. Not because we felt guilty, he had provided us with nothing when he'd locked us in the same place, but we wanted to know that he was still in there.

By the morning, Hugh was completely obsessed with the idea of going home. He didn't believe us, he didn't believe that Alice Tregarthur had gone, but any hope of going home was enough. Whatever hold his step-sister had was losing its power.

But he was shouting when he saw I had his purse of gold coins. 'That's mine, you thief, mine, give it back.'

'Not exactly yours, is it?' I pulled it away.

'We'll need the money for the journey,' Hugh said obviously trying to calm down. 'If you give it to me, I'll get us a fast carriage.'

So, I gave him the purse, didn't seem much point keeping it.

And the carriage was fast, hurtling over the roads, crashing over holes, throwing us around. We stopped to change horses and off again.

'What's the plan?' Hugh said later, as we squashed around a table in Sam and Ivy's house.

Jenna and I were groaning, sick and exhausted by the journey.

'We go home,' Ivy said with just the slightest of catches in her voice.

'But these two,' Hugh said pointing at us. 'These two say you want to stop this by getting all the time travellers back in their own time. Is that right?'

All of us nodded.

'Well, what are you going to do about Masterson?' Hugh looked round at all of us.

'You know about Masterson?' I said.

'I told you, my wonderful step-sister came by recently, she liked to gloat and tell me how everything was working out. Except for me, and she let me know how stupid I was, stupid and useless.' Hugh stopped. He must have had years of torment from Miss Tregarthur, no wonder he wanted to get away.

'Do we need to bother about Masterson?' Jenna said. 'I thought he was living in the right time.'

Masterson had provided us with both problems and help. We had followed Miss T to his houses. He had several, and piles of money, gathered in some way with her help. The year had been 1883. Well, the first year we'd met him; we came back. More confusion, and I didn't want to have to worry about him now.

'He's the reason Alice was able to keep the war going, the one she told me about, something about a never ending First World War. She was really pleased with herself, loved that so many were dead and more would die.'

'Why?' I asked. 'What was in it for her? There had to be something.'

'Apart from being sadistic, murderous, and vindictive, I think she had some idea about world domination. Oh, I missed out crazy. Absolutely crazy,' Hugh looked quite cheerful telling us how awful she was.

'But how did this man Master…what's it, what had he got to do with this war?' Sam hadn't been with us at that time. We hadn't given him all the details of the war. I had hoped we could change time and he'd never have to experience fighting in those trenches.

I had to hope that we were going to send him back to a home, the same sort of place … that made me stop, Sam's parents were both dead, his father killed in a car crash just before Miss Tregarthur took us on her hike. Worse still, his mother had died of cancer before that. Sam had a pile of reasons to be worried about going home.

'Don't you know what's been happening?' Hugh looked pleased that he had something we didn't know. That made me think he would start telling lies, hoping to make some advantage. Although in the end, I think he was just too pleased to tell us the awful story.

'She gave Masterson the plans,' Hugh started.

'We know that,' Jenna broke in. 'She wanted him to make a nuclear bomb, something about getting her crystal to work. She had lost control of the time tunnel and she needed some nuclear power to kickstart things.'

'That was only part of it,' Hugh said, trying to sound so superior. 'Only part of it. That's what she said.'

'And the rest?' I asked, putting my hand over his arm. I wanted him to know there was no option but to tell us.

'Masterson was a German spy,' Hugh said.

'We know that,' Jenna said. 'Tell us something new.'

'Alright,' Hugh looked a bit deflated. 'My step-sister gave him plans to make tanks and guns and rockets and planes. All the things to make sure Germany would win the war and ...'

'But they were only pictures from some encyclopaedia,' I cut in. We had seen the pages Miss Tregarthur gave to this man Masterson, they might provide ideas but none of them told exactly how to make any of them.

'Not the only plans,' Hugh knew this was his big moment. 'She thought you'd find out about the pictures, but you didn't know about the detailed plans.'

'So, Masterson has handed over these real plans for all the weapons to the Germans,' I was getting uncomfortable, squashed up in this room. I had to stand and move to the window. 'But if she did that it hasn't worked. The Germans aren't winning this war, it's a stalemate. And, what's more, I've been in this war and I didn't see these new weapons. Both sides seemed to be using the same sort of stuff.'

'It was enough to stop the Germans losing. Over time, weapon development was not going to work, especially since all the older people were killed off. That's what she told me,' Hugh explained. 'She seemed to like the idea of a never-ending war, I told you she was crazy.'

Jenna called a break, she said she needed a wee, she actually wanted to talk to me outside. Sam and Ivy were trying to get something together for us to eat. It felt as though they needed something normal to happen. Hugh stayed where he was, looking very pleased with himself.

I walked out of the house with Jenna.

'Do we believe him?' Jenna said, as we wandered into the lane.

'Don't see that we have any choice, no one else to ask,' I replied. 'Is it going to make any difference?'

'He's going to persuade us to go to Masterson,' Jenna said. 'That has to be his plan. I'm worried that there is more to his story, that he's up to something.'

I huffed a bit, we talked more, but there wasn't anything we could do differently, so we went back, ate more bread and cheese, and I sat waiting for more from Hugh.

Jenna didn't wait, 'You've been telling us all this stuff, but Masterson can't be responsible for the time mess. The circle of cavemen coming into the world, the disappearance of older adults. That can't have anything to do with Masterson and the war.'

'No, that was all down to my darling step-sister. She just loved messing with time,' Hugh gave a little chuckle, it wasn't the sort of noise that made him any nicer.

But there were many other questions.

'Wait,' I said. 'Miss Tregarthur had lost control of the time tunnel. This loop of bringing the cavemen here didn't start until she had died. Could she really turn up to see you after she'd died? You're making this up.'

Hugh gave me a hurt look, 'You don't know what she can do with time. She's been working on this for years, her and her stupid father. His ideas were even crazier than hers.'

'But this time loop, it's nothing to do with the war, she's done something to time,' Jenna almost shouted. 'You're not telling us everything.'

This was getting too complicated for me. I was feeling that Jenna had to be right.

Hugh was still going on: 'You know it was her sister control-ling time, well they worked on this, she found out there were all sorts of things she could do. Are you sure she's gone?'

I nodded. 'If we believe you, then what are you suggesting?'

'You send me home and then go after Masterson,' Hugh said as though that was the obvious thing to do.

'Or we all go and sort him out.' Jenna didn't seem to think that anything Hugh said was obvious.

'You can't,' Hugh snivelled. 'You promised to send me home, you can't do that.'

'Only problem with sending you home is there isn't one, there is only the war,' I said. 'Is that where you want to go?

Into the war, or since you're older you may just get swapped for a caveman, and we have no idea where you'd go after that.'

Hugh said nothing.

'When do we leave?' Sam seemed to have decided what needed to be done.

'Tomorrow,' I said.

'But it will be just me, Alvin and Hugh who go to Masterson,' Jenna said firmly to Ivy. 'You and Sam go home.'

'But you said we might just be going into a war,' Sam said and nodded to Ivy. 'We'd be safer here.'

'Sam,' Jenna started again. 'We will make it better, we will. We have to. But we can't risk leaving any more people in the wrong time. We believe the time tunnel will make it work for you.'

'And not for me?' Hugh said. 'That sounds more like my step-sister.'

We carried on arguing about that. Eventually all of us found somewhere to lie down and slip into exhausted sleep.

In another early morning, we set off for the Hanging Stones. It wasn't an easy walk. Ivy and Sam barely talked, they might have said they wanted to come with us and help, but it was those two who needed the help. They needed to go home. And as we neared the stones I felt as though Mum knew they needed to go home as well. I just had to hope she could get them to somewhere safe. They had so many issues to sort out.

The blue mist rose up again. Jenna pushed Sam and Ivy into it, preventing us having a weepy goodbye. They were gone. Hugh had tried to follow, but I held him back. The mist changed back to a choking grey and in we went.

16

BLUEPRINTS

'No more deaths,' Jenna said, as the world shook itself back into focus.

The moor looked the same as the one we had just left. It would have been useful if we'd had a clock, not one showing the hours, one showing the years. Was this going to be close to the second time we had chased after Miss Tregarthur and this man Masterson? I felt the tunnel had struggled to tell us what was happening, but nothing seemed to get through. Miss Tregarthur had managed all sorts of things, maybe she had learnt a lot before my mum was swallowed up by this time monster, or whatever it was. At least it was working and we weren't having to use those terrible crystals.

I heard Jenna's words, 'No more deaths.' I repeated them, but I didn't believe it. Death seemed to be linked to everything about time travel and everything we did.

Hugh came out on to the moor slightly behind us. He looked pale and shaken. I had to hope that even if Mum hadn't worked out communication, she had managed to give some people a harder time.

'You got that?' Jenna poked Hugh.

'What?'

'No deaths.' Jenna turned away. 'No more. We've had enough.'

Kan and Posy's deaths had been more awful than anything we had experienced. We hadn't talked about it, even Jack and Mary hadn't spoken of it before they left. I didn't want to go over it now, I was still seeing Kan's face in my sleep. My nightmares seemed to turn around that sword.

'We have to do what we have to do,' Hugh didn't seem to take this seriously enough.

'We've got to get to Masterson, find all these war machine plans, and run for it,' Jenna looked close to attacking Hugh. She might already have decided his death didn't count.

'Whatever.' Hugh moved away.

'We have to get on with it,' I said looking up at the sky. Moorland weather was on its way, we hurried off from the moor.

Jenna and I knew how to get to Masterson's house in London. We would go down to the small town on the edge of the moor, catch a train and then another. Probably take a couple of days to get there.

But as we were coming down from the Hanging Stones I had a feeling we were missing something even more than the whole plot that seemed to be missing all the time. I walked on, trying to remember what it was.

Masterson.

We had last seen Masterson in the back of a carriage at the station. He had come to make sure that we'd captured Miss Tregarthur. We'd chased her to France, in her search for the radiation that ended up poisoning her. We'd brought her back on a stretcher, Masterson came to check. He might have been a part of her plans but he wanted her gone, something he had in common with Hugh.

Masterson was a man of money, his life all set out. He had his big black closed horse carriage driven right down on to the platform, he leant out through a curtained window to get a better look at the sick body of Miss Tregarthur.

What was I missing?

We'd kept to the ridge this time rather than walk down into the valley. It might look a shorter route but somehow shorter distances weren't always the easiest on this moor. In spite of the wind, and then lashing rain, we reached the tor above the village. The one we had seen many times before.

The weather became even worse and we sheltered amongst the rocks.

'Got it,' I said smacking my forehead. 'The cases.'

'Do explain.' Jenna wiped away rainwater from her face.

'He was leaving, when we saw him,' I said. 'That carriage at the station was loaded with cases. He wasn't going to go back to his house at all. He'd packed up everything. He was leaving the country.'

'But we don't know if we are back here at the same time. He could be doing anything. He might not even have got the plans yet.' Jenna didn't seem to feel that this mattered.

'But don't you see?' I held Jenna back. 'Don't you see, it has to be later? If it was earlier then we'd risk meeting ourselves. We know that's deadly, we must be later in time.'

'So?' Jenna. 'We're just getting wetter standing here. Let's go on.'

It wasn't possible to talk through the gale that started. We ended up running down the hill, making for the village, arriving at the Inn.

'You again?' The landlady frowned.

'Yeah, us,' said Jenna. 'And don't try and poison us like you did last time.'

I think the landlady's name was Bettie. I also think she thought we'd come for revenge. She ran, leaving the inn door wide open to the weather. I slammed it shut.

We sat in front of the still smouldering fire, there were no other customers. The old drunks we'd seen before must have left, or drunk themselves to death. We helped ourselves to the beer, it was what everyone drank, but this was terrible stuff.

'1903 it is,' Jenna found a paper on the bar. I wondered how long it had been there. 'What were you on about, seeing cases on the carriage?' Jen asked.

'I don't think he was going to go back to his London house.'

'If he was leaving the country, then we've probably missed him,' Jenna huffed. 'Unless you think we should go off to Germany?'

'No,' I said. 'But I think we should try somewhere much nearer first, we should try his other house. We found one just down the hill from here. Let's try that first.'

'Didn't we nearly get shot there last time?'

'No, I think that was his next big house,' I said.

'We might be wasting time, we might still catch him in London.' Jenna was still squeezing water out of her tunic. 'Surely if you want to get to Germany you'd leave from London. Why would Masterson want to come back down here?'

'Unless he was leaving on a boat from this part of the country,' I said. 'That's where we caught the boats that took us to Australia. Maybe it's easier to slip away unnoticed from here.'

Hugh joined in our conversation. 'We're not going to catch a train this late, might be worth a try at this other house, if it's near.'

Did Hugh have other plans? I wondered how much he might know about Masterson. It seemed Baylock knew about him, perhaps all the Tregarthur people knew about him.

Hugh had been angry that we'd found the few gold coins at his house. Perhaps he thought Masterson might well have more money, even better if he'd left it in a house and disappeared to another country.

Hugh was right about it being too late to get a train and we made the decision to go to Masterson's first house in the nearby village. As we left, we saw Bettie hiding, not very well, behind a tree and getting wet.

'We've drunk all your beer,' I shouted.

'Is that what you did Alvin?' Jenna called out. 'I thought you said it would improve the taste after you'd peed into the barrels.'

We walked on, hearing Bettie screeching. I didn't think anything would have improved the beer or could have made it worse. The rain cleared, as it often did when we walked down from the higher ground on the moor. It wasn't hard to find Masterson's house, he had a preference for large buildings. There were no guards this time, the gate stood open. Going through we could see that the house wasn't empty. The day was ending but still carriages were being loaded at the front of the house. Men shouting to hurry up, everyone seemed to be in a hurry.

'Here to see Mr Masterson.' We'd decided to get Hugh to do the talking to get us inside.

Despite having travelled time and the world, Jenna and I were still teenagers. Having an adult seemed to work. The man at the door just waved us inside. We weren't the only people, others seemed to have come to say goodbye. Masterson was here and leaving very soon. It couldn't be a coincidence that the tunnel had brought us here, just in time. Mum was possibly learning some of the Tregarthur skills.

Once inside the house we were into a mix of people shouting and running about as they cleared the house, and almost a queue to see the Masterson family who seemed to be in a huge sitting room.

'We have to wait,' I said looking at all the people. 'Have to wait until it's quieter, let's get back out.'

'No.' Jenna stopped me. 'It will be harder to get back in. We need to stay inside.'

'Make for the upstairs.' Hugh seemed just a bit too keen.

'Searching for something?' I said.

'Yes,' Hugh didn't feel the need to hide anything. 'This man's got money, he's made it in some scheme with my step-sister.'

'Unlike you?' Jenna said.

'Yes, unlike stupid me,' Hugh answered. 'But I won't feel guilty if we find any of it, and we may still need more money.'

'Where do you suggest we start?' I thought it wasn't a bad idea to look around, we still might have to travel.

'Upstairs.' Hugh looked over his shoulder at the people still waiting to get into the Masterson sitting room. 'We need to check the rooms. If they're all empty then Masterson must be leaving tonight. Otherwise they will be staying.'

Hugh might think himself to be stupid, or actually to be pretty useless, but his idea made sense. It would be much easier if the family stayed tonight. We could wait until the house was empty of other people.

We went up the staircase. Not just your usual stairs. This was a great marble curve of steps leading up to a balcony.

Masterson liked to be grand and this house was nearly as great as the one in London – and probably the same as the others he had.

Upstairs was silent. There were lots of bedrooms and no one around. Most rooms were empty and stripped of everything, except at the front. Two of the bedrooms were clearly in use, boxes of clothes ready to be taken away, but not to be taken immediately.

'Four rooms?' Jenna asked after we'd checked all the other rooms.

'Masterson and his wife, and his daughter will be in the big rooms,' Hugh said. I'd told him about the daughter. I hadn't seen his wife, but there was an older woman with him in the sitting room downstairs. 'The other two rooms are for their staff. They'll be taking them as well.'

'There was another child?' Jenna reminded me.

'Doesn't look like there is a room for another one of them,' Hugh said. 'They wouldn't put a child of theirs into a maid's room.'

'It means there might be more people here tonight,' Jenna said. 'Isn't that going to be difficult?'

'Maybe,' Hugh said. 'But if they are housemaids they won't want to get involved, if there's a fight.'

'No deaths, I told you,' Jenna prodded him.

We slipped into one of the empty rooms at the top of the house and waited. Whatever was happening downstairs went on and on, sounded as though it turned into a party. By the time it went quiet, the light had faded.

Creeping out we heard the family calling goodnight to each other. We had to wait a little longer for the housemaids to take to their rooms. In near darkness, we tried to move silently down the stairs. Light still came from one of the rooms casting a line of yellow from under the door, someone had not gone to bed.

We hadn't planned this. I suppose I was thinking we'd find the blueprints for all the war things: guns, tanks, rockets and whatever. We'd just find them lying about, take them and disappear. I have no idea why I thought that was even likely to happen. But it did. Not exactly like that, but not far off.

'No deaths,' Jenna had stopped in front of the door and waited for Hugh and me to nod. We went in.

It wasn't Masterson's death we needed to have worried about. Inside the room, Masterson sat on one of the few remaining chairs, in front of his desk.

'Come in,' he said. 'Thought I saw you hanging about in the hall.'

The room had mostly been cleared. There were a couple of chairs, a desk and a table with a glass decanter. The last light of the summer's evening still made the dark shapes of trees visible through the uncurtained windows. Most of the light in the room came from a fire glowing in the hearth. Not much warmth came from it, but warmth wasn't needed – this was summer, even if we were still near to the moor.

Masterson sat behind the desk, spread out in front of him were large drawings, the plans we needed. In one hand, he held a glass. In the other hand he held a revolver. I think it might even have been the same gun he had before. He was a very confident looking man.

'I did tell you never to come back again,' he said, sounding like it was such a pity we had not kept away, something that we couldn't have avoided but something that looked like it would have a terrible end. Our end.

'Actually, I thought I would give you another chance,' Masterson said. 'I know my daughter would want me to give you a chance. She's a bit soft.'

'We did save your lives,' Jenna tried a smile, she edged nearer.

'Maybe so, but stand back,' Masterson waved his gun. 'I will shoot, you are obvious burglars. I will be entirely within my rights to shoot you all. But as I said, I will give you a chance. Just leave and nothing will happen, go back to your own time. Vanish.'

'Do you know the war will never end?' Jenna asked.

Masterson shrugged and didn't answer.

'It goes on forever, no one wins,' Jenna added more. 'You must give us these plans and we think we can stop it.'

Masterson gave a false laugh. 'Do I care? We will make some money, piles of it.'

'Sounds good,' Hugh butted in. 'Sounds a very good idea, can I join you?' I believed him, Jenna seemed to as well because she tried to grab Hugh as he stepped forward.

'I can keep Miss Tregarthur away from you if you take me with you,' Hugh pleaded.

'She's dead, why should I care?' Masterson sneered.

I had to hope Hugh was still on our side. His pleading had let him move closer to the desk, it had let us all move a little closer without being noticed this time.

'This is time travel,' I thought it was worth adding. 'She can come back anytime, to check on you.'

I could see Masterson's face crease as he thought about that.

'Now,' Jenna shouted, grabbed the glass decanter and hurled

it at the desk, it broke, smashing the glass into Masterson's face, he howled, I leapt forward. I am my father's son and you don't wait to see what happens to a man holding a gun. Masterson was not able to stop me, blood was in his eyes. I wrenched the gun from his hand.

17

No Deaths

There were noises and shouts from the rest of the house. I was left holding the gun as the door burst open and several people flew in - the family and two men who Masterson must have kept in the house to deal with us, probably to deal with our bodies after he'd shot us.

'Papa,' screamed one of the women, the daughter we had met before, the 'soft' one who became a lot less soft, 'What have you done to him?' she screamed again running towards her father.

'Stop or I shoot,' I shouted. 'Nobody move.'

I heard Jen whisper something about 'no deaths' again – that didn't seem likely. I could see the two men were armed.

We had little chance. I had to steady myself against the desk. Me, Alvin, standing in a room full of people, holding a gun. I needed Dad, the violent drug dealing man who lingered in jail – quite reasonably after the things he had done. But right then I needed him and since that wasn't going to happen, I needed to become him.

I glanced at Jenna and she nodded. She knew my dad, she knew what I had to do. 'Don't move, and no one gets hurt,' I had to cough to stop my voice showing how scared I was. 'You two, drop those guns,' I said to the men. 'If you don't then he gets shot.' I pointed to Masterson, his daughter screamed again.

The men looked uncertain, I moved behind Masterson with the gun at his head.

'Do what he says,' an older woman said, she had to be his wife. 'What do you want?' She said to me.

I didn't answer her question. 'Jenna, get the papers.' Jenna gathered up the plans from the desk.

Ok we had the plans, how were we going to get out of here? I could see that they'd just come after us, we couldn't get back to the Hanging Stones before they caught us. I didn't know what to do. I could see that Hugh was of no use, he was slowly edging towards the door, ready to run. Jenna started feeding the plans into the fire.

Masterson's wife frantically tried to get at her, clawing at the plans. She was a small woman and no match for Jenna who knocked her back to the ground. Why was it her that was so anxious to stop these plans from being burnt?

'You stupid girl,' Masterson's wife cried out, as she picked herself up. 'Those are just a copy, he has more of them. Haven't you?' She turned to her husband.

'No,' he said, sniffing through the trail of blood from his nose. 'They are the only ones. I thought it best to destroy the rest.'

'WHAT?' Masterson's wife went berserk, her face screwed in a hideous grimace. She hurled herself at Jenna again. Jenna shoved her fist into the face of the woman, grabbed her hand, twisted her around and threw her across the room. She bounced on the floor, groaning.

Jenna was not going to be stopped. This was our only chance of stopping the war. If Jenna hadn't stopped his wife I am sure I would have shot her. There was so much anger in this room, mostly mine. We couldn't let Masterson take these plans away.

One at a time the flames roared up. I think Jenna had worked out that there was no way out of here. The best we could do was destroy these plans and give up. I would have to shoot Masterson, we couldn't really be sure that he didn't have other plans, other ideas. I wasn't sure I could do it. Could I really shoot this man? I'm afraid the answer was – yes.

'Jenna,' I stuttered. 'It can't be done without deaths. We can't leave him. I have to do it, he has to die.' I checked the gun was ready to fire.

'No,' his daughter shouted. 'No, take me.'

Masterson's tried to get up. 'You're not going to do that. I won't let you.'

I waved the gun again and he slumped back on the chair holding his nose. I think my sneer must have shown how pathetic Masterson's attempt had been. But, of course, Masterson definitely wasn't the bravest of people.

'You don't need to kill him,' Masterson's daughter pleaded. 'Just take me and no one will follow you, you can escape, you've done what you needed to do, destroyed these awful plans.'

I looked at Jenna and she nodded. I thought the idea might work. But something niggled me – why did she call them 'awful plans'?

Jenna finished burning the papers. Could we believe they were the only plans? Did anyone else know about them? I guess we had to believe that Masterson would have wanted to keep quiet about them, at least until he was in another country. If anyone here knew what he was trying to do, then surely they would have stopped him? Anyway, it seemed he would get to Germany then negotiate with the plans, he needed a nice expensive place to hide – from a war that would never end.

Did he really know that? This pathetic man was going to see so many people die. He was going to let Miss Tregarthur do her worst.

But we were still here. I had done with bravery and hoped Jenna would take over, and she did.

'Great idea,' Jenna said to the daughter. 'We leave together, nobody gets shot.'

Masterson just groaned. He held a handkerchief to his bleeding face. Masterson wasn't going to do anything. He'd used his daughter last time. We'd been captured in his London house with a riot on the street and a performing bear sent though the front door to kill us all. Masterson had pushed his daughter in front of him, she'd just been a child. Still made me wonder what had happened to the other child. The daughter was older in this time and braver than her father. And it was her that sorted things out.

She made all the other people leave: 'Take my *mother* away,' she said to the one of Masterson's men and pointed at the woman who hadn't moved from the floor. Her daughter made the word 'mother' sound like an insult.

'Don't follow us,' I said. 'If we see anyone …'

I couldn't actually say I would shoot her, but I had to hope it sounded as though I would.

We started to leave. I kept the gun pointing at the daughter. Hugh came with us but I didn't like the look on his face.

'I can shoot you as well,' I said giving him a wave of the gun.

I don't think he believed me. Hugh whispered in my ear, 'You have to shoot Masterson, we can't leave him alive.'

'No,' I said.

'Give me the gun,' Hugh said. I had never thought Hugh was

the sort of person who could carry out cold-blooded murder. I wondered if there was something else I had missed. What would make Hugh do this?

But Jenna had said 'no deaths' and I wasn't going to change that. And anyway, if we did shoot Masterson then we weren't going to get away unless we shot all of them.

We left the house. There was still enough light to see the path to the gate and the road outside. No street lights but it didn't ever get really dark at this time of year. Not complete darkness, just a damp breeze blowing from the moor.

Masterson's brave daughter came with us. I'm sure she knew we wouldn't harm her. I think she wanted us to get away, we hadn't really done much harm to her father. And we had saved them all from the bear before.

'When do we let you go?' Jenna asked her.

'Oh, any time you like, I'll go and stay with Jess, she's a friend in the next village.'

'You can't trust her, you can't. She'll just run back to the house and they'll be after us, probably are already,' Hugh said, looking back, but we saw no one.

'She knows we aren't going to do anything,' Jenna said. 'I hope this is the last time we need your help.'

The daughter smiled – we never found out her name.

We left Masterson's daughter at the next village, Hugh was still protesting.

Strangely the daughter said as she left, 'I'm glad you stopped them.'

We didn't hang around to ask questions and went as fast as we could up to the moorland village. By that time, the light had completely gone. There was no way we could have made it across the moor. Last time we had crossed the moor in darkness there had been moonlight and even so we wouldn't have done it – except for the baying, howling villagers who were going to burn us to death if they caught us.

'We have to wait for light,' Jenna said.

'The inn?' I said pointing at the building with light showing in one window.

We were too exhausted, wet and hungry to resist. We went in, the landlady gave a shriek when she saw us again, but we said we wouldn't cause any trouble.

That might have calmed her except I waved the gun, saying: 'That's unless you try to poison us again.' And with that she fainted.

We found something to eat in her disgusting kitchen and tried the beer again, not any better. Jenna did eventually calm Bettie after she'd recovered from fainting.

'Rooms,' Jenna demanded and we spent the night in the rooms we had used in a time before. Hugh took the room Miss Tregarthur had once used. Jenna and I stayed together. I had the feeling that if we really did sort out the mess of time and returned home, no one was going to ever let us spend the night together again. I think Jenna might have thought that as well. We woke in daylight and didn't hear a thing during the night.

'Hugh's gone,' Jenna said in the morning after looking for him in the inn.

Was it happening again? Someone slipping away to stop us having any chance of success. Last time we had Miss Tregarthur with us, supposedly dying of radiation sickness. And Demelza.

We saw the very worst of Demelza, she had slipped out of the inn during the night along with Miss Tregarthur, heading for the time tunnel. But before they left, they'd arranged for the landlady to poison us.

But that time Jenna had expected them to escape – it had been part of Jenna's plan and it worked. This time there was no plan that I knew of, was there?

'And the gun,' I said. 'Hugh must have got into our room while we were asleep.'

'Didn't notice,' Jenna tried to grin. Ah, so maybe she did have a plan.

'Why?'

'He must have gone back to kill Masterson,' Jenna said. 'No point in going after him, it's done.'

'I don't understand why Hugh felt it was so important to kill him.' I checked our room again just to make sure the gun was gone. 'And I didn't think Hugh was up to murder.'

'Neither did I, but, why would we?' Jenna said. 'Why would we be able to decide if someone was going to commit murder? Hey, can all the other teenagers do that? Did they teach us mind reading at school? Did I miss that?'

Jenna sat heavily on the bed. I hugged her.

'I can't take any more of this,' Jenna's head slumped forward into my chest.

'Maybe we've done enough.' I'd held that hope so many times since we'd set off on that school hike with Miss Tregarthur. Hadn't I done enough? I had ended up making decisions, leading people, taking charge. At school, I was more likely to be the cause of everyone's problems, not their solutions.

'Doubt it. Doubt we've ever done enough,' said Jenna, pulling away from me and laughing in a slightly weird way, we were both going a little crazy.

'Why don't we go down stairs and try some poison before we set off back to the Hanging Stones?' I opened the door.

'Won't know if it's poison or not – it'll taste the same either way.' Jenna followed me onto the landing.

'But do we have to hang around for Hugh?' I stopped. 'Haven't we got to get him back?'

'I guess we have to hope he turns up at the stones or gets himself killed,' Jenna pushed me onwards. 'Do you have anything that smells of cow dung,' she said to Bettie who was cowering in the bar.

'Don't think we've ever had that,' Bettie said slowly.

'It's what we had last night,' Jenna gave a giggle.

We had to get out of here. Neither of us was going to get more sensible today.

'Oh, that man with you,' Bettie seemed to have got the joke. 'He left in the night.'

'Did he ask you to poison us, like before?' I could see Bettie had no idea why we were making jokes about this. Somehow it was all getting far too stupid. Maybe that's what time travel does to you – scrambles any sense you have in your head. But really, we were just hoping this was nearly over and thinking that it probably wasn't. Any good feelings seemed bound to be smashed. Neither of us felt that Miss Tregarthur was really dead and gone, despite what we had seen.

After breakfasting on whatever it was that smelt of dung, we set out once again for the moor. Leaving the inn, we followed the track up the hill, passing a couple of white stone houses. No sign of the bailiff's house where we had once saved the life of the king. The village had changed over the six hundred or so years since we had last seen it. I shared that thought with Jenna.

Jenna turned to look back. 'Just have to hope we can add another couple of hundred years to that and get back home.'

'I don't think I'm ever going to come back and check this place, if we get home.' I didn't look back and pushed on, we were soon out into the open moor.

I saw something strange in Jenna's eyes, did she think differently?

Later we followed the muddy route up to the Hanging Stones, more a sheep track than anything easy to follow. Were we both thinking the same? That we hoped this could be the last time? I didn't think it would be. Whatever we had done there were still a lot of cavemen in the wrong time. We hadn't got everyone back in the same time. We seemed to have left more dead than we had saved.

Hugh was waiting for us at the stones. He was shouting and hitting the rock with his fist. The gun, broken into pieces, lay on the ground.

'Trying to run out on us?' I asked, he didn't answer.

'There's nothing here,' Hugh said, picking up the largest piece of the gun. 'It wasn't loaded,' he laughed. 'All that talk in Masterson's house and it wasn't loaded.'

Did Masterson know that? Had he really wanted us to take the plans? I wondered if there could have been someone else driving this idea to take them to the Germans. Maybe it wasn't him at all. Miss Tregarthur might have set it up, but was Masterson strong enough to see it through? Was there someone else?

Jenna turned back to Hugh, 'So you took the gun. You were going to kill Masterson, but it didn't work? Wasn't it loaded?' Jenna's mouth curled in a small grin. No more deaths. Masterson hadn't known about the gun, it was Jenna who had removed the bullets.

'No, it didn't work, but you aren't right. I wasn't going to kill him,' Hugh stopped.

'You were going to kill her? Kill his wife. It wasn't him at all,' I said, slowly realising what had been happening.

'You didn't know,' Hugh gave a laugh. 'You didn't know that it was her that had been set up by Miss Tregarthur. It just had to be the man who looked as though he was in charge, wrong time in history for a woman to run this.'

'Were there more plans? Had they made more copies?' I asked.

'Maybe,' Hugh said. 'Masterson was doing everything his wife told him to do. He must have changed his mind at the end.'

'So, you didn't kill her.' I could see Jenna wasn't sure.

'Didn't have to, she was dead when I got back to the house.' Hugh spread his hands in a hopeless gesture. 'She was lying on the floor with her head bashed in. Blood everywhere. The rest of the family had left. The house was empty – except for the body.'

'He killed her?' I wasn't sure I believed that.

'Him or someone else in the family,' Hugh said.

'Not her daughter, surely?' That seemed so unlikely that the daughter would have killed her own mother. There might have been another child, but we didn't find out.

'Step mother,' Hugh explained. 'Miss Tregarthur set her up as their mother. Masterson was an ideal man for her, weak and desperate for money. His first wife had died, leaving him with the children. Miss Tregarthur helped them, found ways to use her knowledge of history. But it was always the wife.'

I thought of his daughter. The words she'd said. The way she obviously felt about her step-mother. Even if there were more plans I felt the daughter would deal with it. Maybe she hadn't stayed with her friend Jess in the village. Had she gone back to the house? I'd like to think she hadn't actually been the one to do the head bashing in. Or would I? Couldn't say I was unhappy with the result.

Hugh was still looking hopefully at the Hanging Stones.

'Ok, have we done anything to stop the war?' I said, confused and not understanding what was winding me up.

'Hugh, you've not told us everything,' Jenna had picked up my anger.

'And you're not going anywhere until you tell us,' I said, hoping in some way I was talking to Mum.

Hugh laughed, 'You can't control time travel, my Alice said she'd made sure of that.'

'I think I can,' I spoke directly to the Hanging Stones, hoping for some sign.

The sign came with a tremor from the earth. Jenna grabbed me, we nearly fell. I would have liked a bit more, but that was it.

'Ok, Ok,' Hugh cried out from where he'd fallen. 'I'll tell you. Alice said she needed the war to reach a stalemate, that was the trigger for her to start the time loop, to make that year of fighting go on forever. She needed that stalemate to happen before whatever she did with time was going to work.'

'How?' I asked.

191

'Me? How do I know? Remember I'm the stupid one. The one she said would never get home, she said I didn't deserve to go home, that I was hopeless. But I really don't know how she was going to do it.'

'Does that mean stopping the war, stops the time loop?' Jenna asked.

'Again, I've no idea,' Hugh said. 'But it just might.'

The war was only part of the problem. The moor was overrun with cavemen, and we had no idea how to stop them – maybe even more people from the past would start arriving.

Did I believe anything of what Hugh said? There was no way to check, just hope. Watching the stones, I saw the mist rising again. I wasn't sure what colour it showed. We all walked forward. Something made me stop and hold Jenna back. Hugh went on. Did we need him? Too late, he disappeared with a scream that sounded similar to the one made when David had left. I think my mum may have had revenge in mind again.

It was time for us to leave. When would we arrive? What would have happened?

18

THE SWAMP

Sun and the clearest of blue skies. I had never seen this moor sparkle so much. Flashing glints of light bounced off the stream in the distance. A gentle breeze ran through the heather (yes, Mary, I remembered the name) and swept along waves of grass. Warm, and no sign of the sort of weather we had met so many times before.

I listened for sounds. Did I hear an aeroplane in the distance? I looked for danger, cavemen, angry villagers, horses, sheep. No sheep. Cavemen had probably eaten all the sheep. Wait, was that a movement in the distance?

'Keep down,' I said turning back to Jenna. It was just us two. Jenna was already on her hands and knees scrabbling under a large rock a few yards away from the Hanging Stones.

Above her someone had placed another boulder, with writing: 'Look under the rock below.' With a great big yellow arrow pointing the way.

I thought it unlikely that we would find anything, with a sign like that. Then I realised that this just had to be when the cavemen broke through time. They couldn't read. Whatever was under the rock would be safe. Actually, I thought that the cavemen would probably work out something, not many of the rocks were labelled on this moor.

Jenna pulled out an army backpack. Undoing the top, she dived in and came out holding something. 'Phone,' she called out.

It wasn't locked and opened to our touch. One message: 'Phone me, Harper.'

There was only one number on the call list.

'What?' Jenna asked me. 'Do we phone her?'

I nodded. It was too weird to find ourselves in the middle of the moor, in a time when cavemen might be about and see the phone signal was four bars. It had never been that before. It wasn't like that when we went for the first walk, no signal then. The Americans must have placed a mast near here. Maybe down at the army post we had found by the fence.

'Hi,' Harper answered at the first ring. 'Any luck?'

'Maybe,' Jenna answered. 'What's happening there?'

'Same old war, no change, you've only been gone for a day,' Harper said. 'You need to stay there until I come with the other two. It'll take another day.'

'What about the cavemen?' I asked.

'Stay out of their way,' she laughed. 'Oh, there is some food and stuff under another rock, we put a red dot on it. I think there's a tent, if you feel safe enough to use it.'

'But …'

'See you,' Harper hung up.

It sounded to me that we had failed. No end to the war, no end to the cavemen. Had I been too confident about Masterson's daughter? They had left the house, even if it had been after killing the woman set up by Miss Tregarthur. But perhaps the other Mastersons had decided to take over the plan on their own. Did that mean we might have to go back and travel to Germany to stop this war?

Apart from the fact that I didn't feel I could start again, how was I going to have any effect on a whole country's war plans?

I could see Jenna was having the same sort of thoughts.

'No point in going over and over this. Let's just find what Harper has left for us,' she said, looking for the other rock.

We found the tent and the army rations. We decided to put up the tent and watch it from a way off, to see if it drew anyone out of the moor. Did we trust Harper? She said she was bringing the other two. How would she get Zach to come? Did he matter? Couldn't Harper find a way for him to die in this war?

'Wait and see,' Jenna snapped. She was looking at the food Harper had put in a small canvas bag. 'Better,' she said, finding the chocolate. We shared it, not equally.

The day was beautiful. As it ended the moor took on the reds and purples from the setting sun. Slowly the rocky pillars became silhouetted, shadows putting long feelers out over the landscape. The phone rang.

'Sorry, couldn't talk earlier – had to run this country, you know,' Harper sounded cheerful.

Hard to imagine she was still in control. 'How's rat man?' I asked.

Harper giggled. 'He's worse, if anything. I just squeak at him and he hides under the bed.'

'So, you're going to bring him and Demelza up here tomorrow?' Jenna still had chocolate around her mouth. I pointed at it, almost imagining Harper could see her face over the phone, but we were only on voice mode. No other apps.

'Ye...es,' Harper said rather slowly. 'What do you think will happen?'

I had to think about that for a moment. I had a feeling that Harper might not really care what happened.

'Are you coming, as well?' I thought that if Zach and Demelza and we were slaughtered by cavemen, that it might not be too bad for her.

'Is it worth it?' Harper asked, and that confirmed to me that I was right. Death was still on the agenda.

'Has nothing changed at all?' I heard the desperation in Jenna's voice.

'No,' Harper replied. 'Should anything have changed?'

'We managed to destroy the plans,' I said, to silence.

'What plans?' Harper said eventually.

I realised that we hadn't gone into detail about Masterson. Actually, we hadn't known everything about him when we met Harper. We were just trying to escape the war. So many things had happened since then – since yesterday according to Harper's time. If the war was still going on, what had happened to the others we had sent into the time tunnel? I hoped Mum had a way to sort that out, we definitely didn't.

Jenna started to give more detail, but the phone battery wasn't going to last long enough to explain that sort of story. 'Have to tell you the rest when we see you,' Jenna said and hung up.

We watched the tent for a little while longer. No cavemen appeared, the moor stayed quiet, so we climbed into it.

'Don't,' Jenna grabbed my hand as I was about to turn on the torch that came with the army rations. 'We still don't know who is out there.'

In the morning, the clear weather didn't last. No rain, just grey skies and a mist over the hills. We'd pitched the tent in a group of rocks quite a way from the Hanging Stones. In the morning I looked around. These stones had obviously been part of a building. Around us were the remains of ancient walls. Buildings from a long time ago.

'Is this the place where we saw the wild dogs?' I said.

Jenna looked at the remains of the houses, 'Could be, at least there don't seem to be any dead bodies.'

That had been the time of the Black Death, we'd found a pit of dead bodies. Might be ours soon was something I didn't say.

The moor was still so quiet. We went back towards the Hanging Stones, finding a place to hide just a little distance away. There were too many things to worry about.

'Is she going to fly them in on one of the American helicopters?' I asked, but we hadn't seen anything flying since we had arrived.

'She may not want to make this too open, not wanting to let her Americans know what's going on.' Jenna stopped. 'Although I can't see why that would be true. Surely she could claim that stopping the war was all because of her.'

'Not if we haven't stopped it, she wouldn't want to claim a disaster,' I said. 'We have no idea how sorting Masterson might make any difference.'

'Hugh said that Miss Tregarthur used the plans to make sure the war went on forever, that helped her to make this time loop,' Jenna went over the things Hugh had said. Neither of us trusted or believed him.

'But if destroying Masterson's weapon plans was going to work, surely it should have happened already. The war should have stopped.' This just felt like another failure.

Something made me look around. Behind me two soldiers stood, two armed soldiers. These weren't the young teenagers we'd met before. These were two much older men, with a stars and stripes badge on their chests. But camouflaged and arriving so silently.

'Americans,' Harper said as she emerged.

Behind her, still coming up the hill, we saw Demelza and Zach with more soldiers. Difficult to tell if they were coming voluntarily or if they were captives being pushed towards us.

'Is this going to work?' Harper looked at the Hanging Stones. 'Is everything going to be wonderful?'

'If it doesn't work, what are you going to do?' I asked, feeling there was a lot more behind her questions.

'Doesn't really matter to us,' Harper explained. 'We've decided to give up on you, on Britain. If you haven't stopped the war then we are just going to leave.'

'What about the cavemen?' Jenna turned on her. 'You're going to let everyone die, either killed in the war or murdered by cavemen.'

'Well that makes it really important that you've succeeded,' Harper said. 'Anyway, about the cavemen – perhaps you'd better ask them.' Harper pointed into the distance.

Below the Hanging Stone hill a small stream ran down to the valley. Across the stream the ground sloped up to another ridge. The sun was just starting to break through and shine on the crest. That wasn't the only thing lit by the sun.

There must have been more than a thousand of them. They lined the ridge, a thousand cavemen. Well, not just cavemen, some cave women as well.

'No children,' Jenna whispered to me. This felt like a time to whisper. More and more of them were appearing. Like a gigantic wave, they all started to move forward, coming down

198

towards the stream, coming towards us – no noise. Then they stopped again, watching.

Harper was on her mobile calling for help, calling for a helicopter.

'They're not coming,' Harper broke the silence with a shout. 'Not coming. No one is going to come.'

'Sounds like your Americans have pulled out already,' I said, thinking that Harper had been left on her own. Perhaps taking over her Viscount position meant she became too visible. Perhaps the Americans thought it was easier for us all to disappear along with a few soldiers.

'Hello Zach,' I said as the soldiers arrived and delivered the other two. Zach was handcuffed, Demelza had been laughing until she saw the cavemen.

'Alvin, get us out of here,' Demelza demanded.

Clouds gathered, more rain was on its way. We'd had our turn of sun, the real weather would be on us, for the last time.

'Might as well set him free,' Harper told the soldiers to release Zach from his handcuffs. He wriggled out and made for the Hanging Stones, pleading for them to take him away.

'Might be a good idea if we all disappear in your time tunnel,' Harper said, not realising that we wouldn't be able to take her.

The American soldiers stayed with us, checking their weapons. They were proper soldiers, not kids in the trenches. Had we done anything? Had we changed the history that Miss Tregarthur had made?

The cavemen started to move again. A slow and relentless progression down towards the stream, the first of them were starting to reach a swampy area, that wouldn't stop them. Soon they would be coming up our hill.

This wasn't a Miss Tregarthur moment. I liked to think my mum had become a different spirit in the time tunnel. There was a lot of stuff from the past that made me question that. Like why was she so prepared to run off and leave me with the aunt that didn't want me? And what about David? What was he doing with Mum? I guess I knew that, but why and what happened? I tried not to think about my brother.

This still wasn't a Tregarthur moment, no earthquake, no storm. It was as though the air turned thicker, it was harder to breathe, the moor seemed to go out of focus, there were blurred images in front of me. I tried to move, and it happened in slow motion.

'Do we run?' My words came as slow echoes from my mouth.

We stayed where we were. There was nowhere to go.

The cave people were still coming down the hill, moving as though weighed down, each step an effort. Was it the weight of time? Reaching the swamp, they started to sink, fading as they sank, more and more of them came down from the hill. Where had they all been hidden? Every one of them sank into the swamp. They weren't drowning, or struggling, just fading as they came. None of them stopped, just a slow procession.

Then there were no more. The cave people vanished, I had to hope they had returned to their own time. Had Mum managed to do this? Had we helped by making sure the weapons didn't get into German hands? Had we done any good?

I turned to Viscount Harper, but she too was fading along with her soldiers. She gave a smile as she vanished completely, disappearing from the moor, disappearing from our time, I hoped. Was it all over? Could we go home? What had happened to all the other people who had disappeared in some time exchange for the cavemen? Had they all returned? We were never going to find out.

This time it was the world that changed. We didn't move into any mist. Whatever was happening did so around us and I wasn't sure what it was.

There was only a moment before the firing started.

'NO,' I cried seeing flashes in the distance before I heard the crash. Tens of guns were firing, I could see the shells hurtling across the moor, crashing into the rocks, some coming our way.

'Run,' I shouted. At least we could move.

'Wait,' Jenna called again. 'They aren't shooting at us, something else is happening.' Demelza and Zach were still there, holding on to the Hanging Stones.

Was it something I said or felt or thought? No words, but something inside my head made me think that Demelza and Zach could leave, the mist rose from the stones, gathering around them, and they faded like the others had done, but I think I heard a scream – were those two in for a hard time traveling experience to wherever they had gone?

Jenna was shielding her eyes, trying to see what was happening in the distance.

'It's still war,' she said. 'I think those are army guns practising. I thought it was over.' Jenna sank to the ground. 'No good.'

It didn't feel like that to me. I was sure something had changed, we'd seen the cavemen leave, hadn't we broken Miss Tregarthur's endless war?

'We have to go over there and check,' I said.

201

'Great idea, Alvin,' Jenna said, sitting on the wet grass with a look that seemed to say it was the end of the world and she'd given up. 'Great idea, walk over to where they're firing guns. I suppose it could be an easier death.'

'Jen, get up,' I stood over her holding out my hand. 'We can do this. So many things we've beaten, just a few guns are simple.'

Jenna got up, looked me up and down. 'Alvin,' she said. 'There is something very different about you, if we ever get back home I don't think you'll fit in at all.' She laughed, we both laughed and walked in a wide circle away from the direction the guns had been firing.

The moor wasn't silent for many minutes. There was more gun firing and we heard shouting. As we made our way to another tor peak we could see what was happening. The guns were all firing at a target, and not doing very well. It looked like some sort of gun practice. We seemed to be on a firing range. We stopped and watched. We tried to talk, but the noise was too loud. It was too loud to talk and too loud to hear the noise of an army truck coming over a moorland track and stopping just below us. We didn't hear them but we saw the soldiers get out and run towards us pointing their guns.

'Men,' Jenna shouted over the noise.

They were men. Not teenage soldiers. Men, not children or teenagers or anyone who looked young.

The firing stopped, it seemed that the practice was over for the day, we could see the soldiers hauling the guns over to the back of other trucks and being driven off.

'You two are trespassing,' said the soldier in charge. 'Didn't you see the warning flags, are you stupid?'

I nodded, feeling very stupid.

'Wait a minute, boy.' He stared at me. 'You're in uniform, must be a deserter, run off with his sweetheart?'

The soldiers all laughed at that.

'Any chance you could answer a stupid question?' I asked.

The soldier looked puzzled, he must have expected me to be scared. Strange how many death defying moments made this seem quite unreal.

'Any chance you could tell us what year it is?' Jenna asked the question for me.

That clearly identified us both as mad and probably bad.

'Get them in the truck,' the soldier said.

'Yes, Sarge,' saluted another.

We were dragged off to the truck and bundled into the back.

'You're in real trouble,' one of them said. 'But it's 1919 if you want to know.'

'What was it last year?' I tried another stupid question.

'1918,' the soldier said. 'You trying to make fun of me?'

We both shook our heads and smiled. I wanted to ask about next year but thought that was a question much too far. The jeep drove off up to an army camp. We'd never been in this direction on the moor. I had no idea there was a camp here.

'It's the normal war,' Jenna laughed. 'We've done it.'

'Nothing normal about war, girl,' the Sergeant said in a firm army voice. 'How old are you?'

We gawped at him. How old was I? How old was Jenna?

'You from that loony bin?' another soldier called out. 'You know Sarge, that place down in the town where they keep all the ... what's its. Maybe that's where she's from.'

I was worried that Jenna might start on him for talking that way about mental health. Jenna would have been right but somehow this wasn't the time.

'They shoot deserters,' said the soldier who'd told us the year. He raised his fingers gun-fashion at my head, 'BANG. Especially those running off with girls.' He tried to give Jenna a pinch, bad idea, I don't think she actually managed to break his nose. They didn't talk to us after that.

Back at the camp, I was marched off to yet another army cell in one of the single-story buildings. There was no one else in the cells, but room for a lot more. Through the bars, I could see the soldiers covering the guns they'd brought back from the firing range. I heard Jenna being told to run off. It was only me that was in trouble.

Another death threat moment, just as we seemed to have broken the never-ending war loop. I had thought we'd finished with anything awful Miss Tregarthur could throw at us, I was obviously wrong.

A little while later more soldiers arrived. One who looked more important looked me over. 'Which brigade?' he said.

I was trying to remember what Jack had said when we were on our way to the front before. He'd looked at the badge on my shoulder. It was some number. I couldn't remember what.

'6th, Sir,' one of them said. 'Badge on his shoulder, 6th Brigade.'

'So, you ran?' the captain almost looked sad. 'How did you get away?'

'On leave, sir.' I tried a salute and managed to poke myself in the eye. It wasn't a good story.

'It'll be a court martial, tomorrow, then …' he stopped.

'You're going to shoot me?' I asked, trying to keep the shake out of my voice. Was this the time to tell him I was from the future? Somehow, I thought that might make it even worse. They left. I was given something to eat. All those who came to my cell had long sad faces. I had the feeling they had seen other deserting soldiers being shot.

Night came.

'Get in the corner,' I heard her whisper through the bars.

'What, how?' I whispered back.

'Shut up and move,' she said slightly louder. I moved.

Of all the things I had seen this had to be the most unlikely.

I was sure that Jenna had been working on a farm when we had been dragged into Miss Tregarthur's endless war. After I had been taken to the front, Jenna and Demelza had been sent to a farm. What she'd left out was what they were doing on the farm other than farming. Something to do with testing and packing explosives, she told me that later.

The exploding shell took out the wall, the bars, an old desk in the corridor, and the wall on the other side. The noise deafened me. I saw Jenna peer in through the hole, waving frantically. We ran as the army camp erupted into action.

'Alvin, just hide.' Jenna pulled me to one side by a truck. 'I'll drive off, they'll follow. Just make sure you get back to the Hanging Stones.'

There was no time to ask her how she managed to blast me out of jail with the huge army gun, nor how she'd got the keys to this truck. I grabbed her, held her in a kiss.

'Get off, idiot.' I could see Jenna's smile in the dim glow of lights from around the camp. More lights were coming on. More shouts, and whistles.

I wanted to go with Jenna but she took off, driving wildly

down one of the tracks. Why hadn't I gone with her? I disappeared into darkness. It took a few minutes before the army camp got moving, but soon other trucks were being driven after her. I had to hope she had a plan, I wasn't going to wait to find out. I ran quietly in the opposite direction, towards the Hanging Stones.

-19-

JACK'S BLUE

The track showed as a faint trail of silver in the near darkness, not easy to find as I ran, often stumbling to the side, falling into a ditch or gorse bush. In the distance, I could hear the army vehicles, engines revving as they chased after Jenna. I should be with her, I thought, feeling useless and stupid.

The crash echoed across the moor. One of the trucks must have turned over. I saw lights shining into the sky, then a sheet of flame as it caught fire. Had that been Jenna? Had she been killed in the crash? I had to find out. I ran back across the moor, no path, a dangerous route through boggy, stony ground. The sort of route that the mob had chased us along before, wanting to carry out their death sentence. I had to keep low, there was very little moon, but it would be easy to be silhouetted as I went up another slope. Below me I could hear shouts, cresting the hill I saw the army vehicles parked with their headlights shining down over small cliff, further away the burning truck. It had to be Jenna's. I started to go nearer.

I heard another shouted voice, seeming to come from the crashed truck. I went closer. The soldiers were starting to look around.

'There's no one in it,' I heard another shout. 'The boy must have legged it.'

'Soon get him,' another shout. 'Sarge is bringing the dogs.'

Was Jenna in the crashed jeep? Or had she escaped? I wanted to go down and find out. But I would get caught and if Jenna had managed to escape everything would have been useless. I didn't think Jenna would get another chance with any of the army's big guns. I couldn't stay but I wanted to watch a little longer. Dawn was coming, a grey light in the sky. Soon there would be no cover, and dogs. The soldiers had moved away from the crash. They were waiting for others to arrive and start searching. I had to go, hoping this was part of Jenna's plan.

In that first light, I could see I was on the tor above the village we'd been to so often. I took off, running in a crazy dangerous way, hurtling across the moor, tripping over stones, falling to ground, picking myself up and running again. I had to see if Jenna had made it, otherwise I would go back and give myself up. No point in anything without Jenna.

I wouldn't need to give myself up. In the light from the rising sun I would soon be seen as I charged along the ridge. I heard barking in the distance. I heard shouts. They were after me.

I made it to the end of the valley and started up the muddy track. I could feel the burn in my throat as I gasped for each breath. On I went, shouts from behind getting louder. My mind suddenly flashed with the memory of the crazed mob that had once chased me. At least these soldiers might not burn me to death.

They wouldn't need to. In the distance, I heard a shot. The soldiers had reached the ridge. Was I in range? They might be old guns in my real time but for these soldiers they were modern weapons. How far could they shoot?

I made the final distance and collapsed beside the Hanging Stones. More shots. I think I heard a bullet hit something below me. It wouldn't be long.

Breathless I staggered up. The sun broke through, shining on the Hanging Stones. I collapsed beside them, panting and looking back to see if I had been followed. To see if there was any sign of Jenna.

I could feel a pull from the stones, as though I was being dragged towards the time tunnel. I could leave, perhaps they would shoot Jenna for helping a deserter. Then it wouldn't matter that she didn't get home. I wasn't going to leave her. I would have to go back. I would give myself up to the soldiers when they reached me. I had to hope they would know what had happened to Jenna. Would they tell me before they fixed up a firing squad?

I didn't care if the bullets got me. I stood up and started shouting, 'I'm here,' I shouted again as I started to walk down the hill.

'Where do you think you're going, soldier?' came her voice. 'Are you thinking of running off with your sweetheart?'

How long had she been watching me? I fell into her, squeezing her so tight. My Jenna, my hero.

'I'm not going to keep saving you when we get home,' Jenna said pulling me back to the Hanging Stones.

'How?' I pulled back.

'Which of the hows do you want me to explain?'

'All of them,' I said.

'No time for that.' Jenna pointed down at the soldiers. They were charging towards us. There were more shots, and we could definitely hear the crack of bullets hitting the stones below.

But with Jenna beside me, this didn't feel so bad. Something was very different up here on the moor. I wasn't scared. It was almost as though there was laughter in the air, was that my mum? A shimmering blue mist rose from the stones, covering us. We were on our way.

Noises, sirens, lights, whistles, the whirring of a helicopter. Blue lights lit the moor. Jack had described this, he'd met this scene when the time tunnel had once returned him home from the caveman world. This blue came from flashing lights. A full-on moorland rescue with police, army, ambulances, news media – and parents. A crowd had gathered at the bottom of this Hanging Stone hill.

'This way, kids,' shouted someone who seemed to be in charge of a group of rescue volunteers. We were led down the hill. As we appeared the crowd below started to run towards us.

I stumbled forward, it wasn't just me and Jenna. There were others from the walk, Miss Tregarthur's hike into time. I held Jenna's hand, but already I could see questions on her face. Jack had said when he had returned, that memories of our time travel seemed to disappear like dreams. Jenna pulled away as though I had done something wrong, as though she hadn't been with me through all the dangers we had faced.

Was this the same for everyone – except me? My mind wasn't blank. Everything was in sharp focus, from the time we started on that first hike all the way through the disasters, and how we had survived.

We fell into the rescue. Making the bottom of the hill, it was an adult world that took over. Jenna was taken away, wrapped in a foil blanket, fussed over. I saw her confused face, she shot me a glance, perhaps not everything had faded. But no one was going to let any of us make decisions – like running, escaping from murderous crowds of villagers, sailing across oceans. Our decisions were whether we wanted a cup of tea, biscuits, to lie down.

We had disappeared on Miss Tregarthur's hike. This rescue seemed exactly as Jack had described it, his first rescue. A replay for Jack. I even heard him asking how long they had been looking for us, and someone saying they had been looking all day.

As the sirens blared and the helicopters whirred above, I heard them use the word – earthquake. It seemed that they knew about the earthquake. But like on Jack's first return, not every one of us had made it, not everyone had survived.

In this misty confusion, shouts and screams became the loudest noises. Parents of those children who were nowhere to be found.

'Stop, stop,' howled one mother. 'Tell us what happened. Where's my Sara?'

I wanted to tell her, how she'd fought and lost the battle with food poisoning, how we had buried her under a mound of earth. I stepped forwards.

'Carter, where are you going?' came a familiar loud voice. I recognised the head teacher, he usually shouted at me. 'You need to watch that boy.' I was moved away. I suppose my history, Alvin Carter – bad boy, bad family, bad everything – I suppose that stopped people asking me anything, or at least believing anything I might have to say. I had to sit and listen. I got a blanket, but no tea.

'Find them, find them,' came another howling voice.

'What are you doing?' a man shouted. 'Let me go, get off, I have to …'

His voice trailed off. I could see a line of police holding parents back, stopping anyone trying to get back up the hill.

Down from the high moor, at the stream, four-wheel drive vehicles had made it along the track – army vehicles. Further away I could see other normal ambulances. There was no escape from this, but at least they weren't going to kill us – yet.

So strange to be taken over by other people. I couldn't cope.

I saw Zach. I leapt up.

'You.' I threw off my foil safety blanket and charged forward. I was going to strangle him.

Perhaps the mist of our travel in time lifted from Zach at that moment. I saw someone, was it Mary or Jack or Demelza or even Jenna? Difficult to tell under the foil blanket wrapping. But I saw someone whisper in Zach's ear. And before I could get to him he went berserk – smashing his way through the helpers, knocking over a film crew, trying to barge through the police line.

'NO, NO, KEEP THEM AWAY,' Zach screamed at he tried to swipe away imaginary rats on his clothes. His screech seemed to stop everyone.

His parents were there, ordinary people, not parents who would ever think they had made this murderous monster. They ran after him, tried to calm him. Zach wasn't to be calmed. He fought against everyone, still brushing something away, something only he could see. I didn't need to strangle him – his mind was full of the rats that drove him mad. Zach was tackled to the ground, a nurse stood over him shouting for the doctor, who appeared and injected him with something. His parents helped carry the unconscious Zack to an ambulance.

I didn't see him again after that moment, but it was a scene that changed everything. Parents became quieter. Reunited families grouped together and were taken away. The parents of the missing were isolated, standing alone on that windswept moor. The parents of: Sara (other Sara as we called her) poisoned by an uncooked chuckern; of Ben who had been killed by a sabre tooth tiger; and Ryan who had died in the trenches of Miss Tregarthur's war.

No one was there for Kan and Van. That hit me hard. They were a wonderful crazy pair from a crazy family – crazy and dangerous. They had followed us into time to escape something they called 'trouble' but met their deaths through helping us. They hadn't been on the original Miss Tregarthur's walk so there wasn't a welcome party for the two of them. I wasn't sure there was anyone left alive at their home, the 'trouble' could have meant that a welcome party for them might have been really bad news.

No one came for me either. I was almost left behind. I didn't need an ambulance, no one actually suggested that I might need one. Having lost my foil blanket, I seemed to become just one of the crowd of people watching. Tourists seemed to have arrived, walkers off the moor – ordinary folk, from their own time. I could have walked off with them. But my head teacher found me, and suggested to the police that I should be taken away.

'Where to?' asked a policeman.

'Jail, would be a good idea,' the head said. 'He probably was the cause of all this mess.'

'What, the earthquake?' said one of the media people who

had become interested.

The head gave a sigh, 'Maybe even he couldn't do that.'

How wrong they were, but I became uninteresting again. Led away, driven away, I wasn't taken to jail in the end. They drove me back to the house of my aunt and uncle. The police called it my home. I'd forgotten what it looked like, a neat and fussy bungalow with gnomes in the garden. Never my home.

'Brought back by the police, as usual,' my aunt said on the door step. Her arms crossed tightly over her chest and a face that would sour anything. 'Not long now.' She turned away. No sign of my uncle.

I wasn't welcome, but I had come back three days before my sixteenth birthday. I went up to the room I had been given. Three more days of being here before they would throw me out. I knew I had been difficult, and perhaps my aunt had done her best. This wasn't a problem I could solve in any time tunnel.

I collapsed on the bed, burying my head in a pillow that smelt of something my aunt had probably used to get rid of the smell of me. But with too many thoughts filling my head I did not sleep.

It was a strange normality. For everyone, except me, the blankness in their minds meant only the walk and the rescue seemed to matter. The blankness didn't last but at first the others remembered nothing of mammoths, plague, wars or any of the terrible things we had been through.

Being in our last year at school meant most of us weren't expected to return this late in the term. In fact, we wouldn't usually be wanted. Definitely not wanted in my case. Of course, that all had changed after Miss Tregarthur's hike. School was buzzing. Not only that, but all of us who had been on the hike were called in for counselling, on the very next day.

A nice friendly chat with professionals, they said, and compulsory. I just hoped that if the memories returned then Stevie and Matt wouldn't remember everything about the war. Jack too.

They split us up, the few younger students had to return to school classes anyway and they had their own specialist to talk to.

The rest of us traipsed into school. Coming in the back way to avoid the media. They'd been running headline stories since we returned:

'Earthquake takes walkers'; 'School trip disaster'; 'This moor is dangerous'; 'Mystery of the disappeared children', and others.

It wouldn't go on for long. It was difficult to find someone to blame. The school wasn't responsible for earthquakes, they didn't happen, no one could have predicted the loss of life from some natural disaster.

I checked who had come into school with us, Zach wasn't there.

'He's been taken away and ended up in a psychiatric hospital,' Mary reported.

I heard the others talking, it was obvious that some memories were returning. I was left out, as I had been before the walk. I wasn't the sort of person they wanted to talk to.

Demelza arrived. She must have spent the night at a spa, her hair glistened, her nails shone bright red and her face glowed in the way only something expensive could make her glow.

Until Demelza went to the loo. Followed by Jenna, Mary and Ivy.

I knew Jenna was a bit of an expert in doing makeovers, saved our lives before. But I didn't know you could do that with lipstick and stuff.

Demelza looked fabulous – provided you liked pandas who had obviously lost a fight and appeared, from the red streaks, to be bleeding heavily. Also, the toilet flush hadn't actually improved her hair style. Demelza fled. Even the headteacher wasn't going to stop someone looking like that.

We had our counselling session in a group. Someone said they understood how we felt, the trauma, the awfulness. She didn't. She didn't even have a sensible idea how I would find some way to get some sleep. We probably needed pills.

After the session, Jenna came to me. She took my hand and smiled. It wasn't exactly as it had been, but it still felt good. 'Birthday party at Mary's.' She kissed me on the forehead and left.

I didn't care what was going to happen to me. If I could keep Jen then that was all I needed. Of course, Jenna couldn't have a party at her house. I had forgotten how much mess there was in her life – mother, mother's boyfriends and things I had tried to keep out of my head. For me, she was just my wonderful Jenna, we'd been through so much together.

One more counselling session. Jack talked about bears, Matt said something about hunting, Mary told him to be quiet, Sam cried a bit, Ivy held him. Jenna and I just watched as the therapist tried to keep herself together before shouting, 'Why are you doing this? Why are you all telling me these lies?' before she stamped out. That was the end of therapy.

I went to the party with my bag of clothes. My aunt said good riddance, my uncle wasn't there to see me leave. I couldn't think of anything sensible to say when I left, so I told her Miss

Tregarthur would be back and was pleased to see the effect. My aunt obviously knew a lot more than she had ever told me.

At the party, they were all there. The older ones, and a card from Emma, Sara, Zoe and Stevie with a picture of a mammoth on the front. It wasn't a riot. We mostly just sat and looked at each other, occasionally bursting into hysterical laughter. Ivy didn't laugh though.

At the end, after the cake that Mary's mum had made, we started to leave, with promises of meeting again – something that we would never do because this had been too scary, Jenna walked away with me.

'Back to mine,' Jenna said.

'But ...' I looked at her. 'What about your mum? What about her boyfriend?'

'Are you Alvin?' Jenna smiled at me. 'I need you to save me.'

I laughed. It had always been Jenna who had done the saving. She just put ideas into my head.

The next few days didn't exactly pass quietly in Jenna's house. There was a lot of shouting. But I did save Jenna. Because Jenna told them that my dad was coming out of jail next week and if they didn't look after me my dad would probably burn the place down and beat them to death. That was the way I saved Jenna.

Her mum's boyfriend tried to leave, Jenna told me to stop him because he'd pinched the housekeeping money. That was before she tripped him up and took it back. I was very good at saving Jenna. We had all changed.

We talked. A lot. It had been our exam term before we'd left on the hike. Results would come our way soon. Neither of us were expecting prizes. The fact that I had taken any exams was unusual. I hadn't really expected to need those sort of qualifications. I had assumed Dad would take me in on the family business. I think that Miss Tregarthur had provided me with great training for Dad's business. It would be hard physical work – drug running, theft, and violence. I didn't feel as though I would have any choice after Dad got out of jail this time. I had no idea whether he knew about my brother, or even Mum. That they were both dead. But I did know that would mean Dad needed another helper, 'to watch my back,' as he often said. Even if it was mostly watching his front, being in the line of fire.

'Great prospects,' Jenna said, again reading my thoughts – they weren't difficult.

'What about you?' I said, thinking her chances in life weren't really any better than mine.

Jenna looked away. 'We have to go back into school tomorrow, there's going to be a plaque ceremony.'

We went back, already a small group had gathered round the school entrance. On the wall in the foyer a small green curtain was covering something. Three families stood apart, dabbing their eyes, blankness on their faces. The families of the lost. Some man in a suit pulled a cord and uncovered the plaque:

IN MEMORY OF THOSE LOST IN THE DARTMOOR EARTHQUAKE

SARA BENJAMIN

RYAN HOUSE

BEN FINDER

I'm not sure I had ever known their surnames. Probably had forgotten. Ryan and Ben must have been with me for most of my school life. They didn't deserve to die, even if they had taken up with Zach. The ceremony didn't last long. The adults drifted away. Some of us hung around for a while, but we'd mostly stopped talking to each other.

The others might be remembering what happened, but they wanted to forget. It was all too bizarre to believe it had been real. Maybe it hadn't been. Maybe we had been part of some weird experiment, aliens, whatever. Just forget it.

I went to the loo; the female toilet door still had traces of a smeared red colour – or hot blush as Jenna told me was the stuff Demelza used.

Coming out of the loo the school was deserted. That was except for a small sobbing heap under the plaque. Ivy's arm was stretched out, still holding a nail, something she must have picked up from the school building works. She'd scratched on the plaque above her:

Baby Sam

No surname. I took a step towards her, not knowing what to do. Jenna appeared from around the corner. She joined Ivy on the floor, she reached up, handed me the nail and nodded towards the plaque. I scratched Kan and Van Peta's names.

I walked away and didn't look back. There were very dark thoughts in my head.

ONE STONE

'Has to be done,' said Jenna.

'Why?' I didn't look at her.

'You know why.' Jenna pulled me towards her and waited until I nodded.

We planned a bit.

'Any money?' I asked, not having any myself.

'Some £5 notes.' Jenna still had some of the old white paper notes, she had been great at keeping hold of important stuff.

'Can you use them?' I fingered the notes, odd old paper.

'I think you can change them at a bank.' Jenna was holding a note up to the light. 'But you may have to go to London.'

'I think I know a man who might change them for us without going there,' I said recalling Jim who ran a pawn shop in town. Not a very legal sort of place.

We went to see the man. It really wasn't very legal and Jim was very jumpy. But he swapped some of the notes for cash after I told him Dad was coming out of jail quite soon. I rather thought we could have got more, but I am sick of sorting things out. I knew we had to do this, but I didn't want to, I wanted it all to go away.

We caught a train. To Exeter. The line had been closed for the onward journey. We caught a bus.

The bus dropped us at the bottom of a hill.

'Wasn't Masterson's house down there?' I pointed. It didn't really look too different; more houses, a road with cars, but up ahead it looked much the same. We didn't go and look for Masterson's house, this wasn't about him. We climbed the road up to the moor.

'Our school coach stopped here,' Jenna said as we came out on to a village green. Jenna meant the very first bus, carrying our hiking group and … Miss Alice Tregarthur. The squabbling and shouting as we piled out of the coach. The two support mums who had come along, something about their hair, couldn't remember what.

'Up there,' I said, and we walked through the village.

'Church.' Jenna pulled me to the side. We looked over the gravestones – no sign of anyone we knew. No Van or Kan or Posy. They had disappeared with their deaths. We walked on up the hill, through a gate and out onto the open moor.

Ahead a red flag flew at the top of an iron flagpole.

'Eh?' I looked around wondering what it meant.

'It means there is army firing,' said one of two walkers who came up behind us.

'You?' I said quite loudly, recognising them.

Mary and Jack had followed us. They just nodded and we went up the hill towards the outcrop of rocks, the first tor. Sam and Ivy were waiting. I don't think we said anything or I don't remember. I was thinking. Jenna must have told them, told them what was driving me crazy, what I needed to finally sort out.

I hadn't taken any notice of the weather. It was a nothing of a day, cloudy, bit of a breeze but nothing weird, strange or dangerous. I knew it could change. We walked on along the ridge, then dipped down to the stream.

There were still signs left by the vehicles from our rescue. Ruts in the grass, odd bits of rubbish. Mary said she'd pick them up when we came back down.

'I think I should go up there by myself,' I pointed up to Hanging Stone Hill.

'No way,' came their voices.

We climbed together. I had to go over things in my mind. We'd come out of the time tunnel into the rescue. It had happened so quickly, no time to look back, to see what might be happening in this time travelling whatever.

What was this thing on the moor? These Hanging Stones? So many times we had stood before them. Before we had come to them in terrible danger, this time it all felt so different. A bunch of teenagers out on the moor. No cavemen, no death sentences, no sailing trips to the other side of the world. These were just stones, or just one stone.

'It's called a Logan,' Mary said. 'The stone thing, it's called a Logan. But the weird thing is that no one else seems to know about a proper Logan stone on this hill.'

What was it we had seen? Was it only stone? Was it my mum in some form?

If that was the truth, then one day would it be me?

That was the thought that haunted my thoughts.

When I died I would be taken up into the stones, become the spirit in the moor that controlled time. Would someone find a crystal and make me do what they wanted? Would I feel the awful screaming pain we heard coming from the stones, when Miss Tregarthur struck her crystal? Somehow her hate and need for revenge had allowed her to overcome the pain.

And was I the last? Had Baylock and his family all been killed by cavemen? We'd brought back two of Miss Tregarthur's supposed relatives. I didn't think they had been born in the house.

They hadn't been brought into the world surrounded by that green glow of radiation in the Baylock house or cave. They didn't share my destiny, my fate.

The others held back as I approached the stones. They all knew why we had come here. To find out what might happen to me. But they hung back. None of them wanted to travel again in time. It had taken us either thousands of years or just one day in modern time to sort out the mess that Miss Tregarthur had thrown at the world. Her legacy.

I looked at this strange formation of rock, looking as though one stone was balanced on another. Just one stone really, and try as hard as you could, it would not separate. Just one stone. Except that it wasn't. We had seen the stone split in two, becoming a pincer that had reached out for Miss Tregarthur's body, raised it into the air and then dragged her into the moor. How she had been brought back to some form of life, deep within the rocks, the granite rocks – I remembered someone telling me they were granite.

Looking at the Hanging Stones I knew it would happen to me. I could feel the draw of the moor. I would not escape.

'Get to another country, it can't get you then,' Jenna had said but I knew that would never happen. I would never be able to move away. I would be pulled back here; the force was too strong. It would all start again with me. Someone would find a way, I would travel them in time. New disasters would happen and it would never stop for me. There was no one else who could take my place. I could never leave the rocks of Dartmoor once I died. This would be my burial, dead but not dead – for ever.

A mist curled up around the stones. The tunnel was opening. If I stepped forward I would be taken again. I looked back. Jenna's face screwed up. I knew she would want to come with me, but it was too much. All of us wanted to live our lives out in our own time, no Black Death or hangings or convict ships across the world. Just to be ordinary. I wanted that too, I did not want to go anywhere.

'Come,' I heard my mother's voce. Not a real sound, but the word came into my head.

I didn't move. This might be my mum but I didn't feel I could really trust her. She'd run off, left me, brought Miss Tregarthur into my life, seen my brother die. But Mum was in my head. She could feel my thoughts and I could feel her sorrow, the regret she had for all the things that had happened. The things she felt she had done.

'Come,' came her call again. I turned back to the others, gave a shrug which I hoped meant I had no choice and I stepped forward.

The stones of the moor opened to let me in. I felt as though I had entered a cave. There had been caves once before. But this was different. So many colours surrounded me, purples and greens and blues, all the colours we had met before in the mist of this time travel, but I wasn't moving, there was no swirling vortex to take me.

'You must go to him.'

I felt those words. I knew what it meant. She meant my dad. I had to go to him, tell him about my brother; about Mum. I had to do it. I had no idea what would happen, what Dad would demand, whether I could escape the life he might drag me into, but I had to go.

'There will be no more,' Mum's voice sounded more like the one I remembered, even though she'd not done a lot of mothering, it was a voice from long ago, a voice to the child I had once been. 'It will stop with me, I will make it stop, there will be no more.'

I could feel the wrench. Mum was going to bring the time tunnel to an end. She had found a way. Miss Tregarthur's way had been to wreck time, Mum had found a way to stop this. It would not be my fate. But Mum would be no more. I understood that, she would die a real death, not be a spirit forever living on in the moor. But was I ready to let her go? There were so many things I wanted to understand, so many things that Mum might have told me. Maybe I could travel again in time and change our family.

'NO.' Mum would not let that happen. 'No more. You must let me go.'

Let her go? At first I couldn't understand, what did I have to do? Slowly it came to me. I was already part of this, I had found the tunnel on the first day and found it again at other times. It hadn't been coincidence, I was part of it.

'You must say the words.'

How did I know the words? If I knew them, did I want to say them, did I really want to see the true end for my mother?

'You must say them.'

I knew what Mum meant. The words that Baylock had used. I didn't understand how I had remembered them, but I had.

'By the stones, by the earth, by the water, I call upon you to stop, to return to peace.' I cried.

'Again,' Mum's words were soft in my head.

'By the stones, by the earth, by the water I call upon you to stop, to return to peace.'

I felt the world change around me, slipping out from this cave, moving through the earth and stone. I was back on the moor.

Slowly a deep mist rose up around us. I could barely see my hands in front of my face. This wasn't the mist of the time tunnel, this was a true Dartmoor mist. No earthquake this time but a deep rumble came from far below, rising up through the Hanging Stones, a rushing sound spreading across the moor, and finally a sigh that told me this was over.

Jenna caught me as I started to fall.

'It's over,' I said. She nodded.

The others surrounded me. I held on to Jenna, waiting in case something more would happen, something terrible that would plunge us into the disasters of time. But it didn't. It was the end, there would be no more of Miss Tregarthur, her promises, her crystal, we would never be her prisoners again and she would not have her revenge. It was over.

But it was more than over. The moor hadn't changed but there was something missing. The balanced stones that had been the sign of the time tunnel had vanished. There was a stone. A stone that hung out over the moor. The real Hanging Stone, one stone that would mark this place forever.

EPILOGUE

'He's changed,' I told Jenna after visiting Dad in jail.

'How?' She asked. 'Is it good?'

'He's giving up crime, taken up training in there.' I stopped. 'He's going to become an accountant.' I felt the embarrassment. Somehow, I felt being an accountant wasn't actually much of a change.

'And?' Jenna knew there was more.

I coughed. 'He says I have to go to college.'

Jenna laughed, gave me a poke. 'We could go together.'

I paused, looked away.

'You don't fancy trying a walk on the moor?'

www.cillianpress.co.uk

ABOUT THE AUTHOR

This is Alex Mellanby's fifth novel to complete the current Tregarthur Series. He has never been lonely in his writing, sharing the task with his characters. Alvin is now a very different, Jenna has made all of them better people than they were when they set out on this Dartmoor hike. Ivy is still miserable, but she has a lot to cope with, not the least being me, the author.

www.tregarthurseries.com

Join in on the conversation at
facebook.com/tregarthurseries